11 Bodies Moving On
(a Body Movers novel)

STEPHANIE BOND

CHAPTER 1

CARLOTTA WREN stared at the locker that had been hers for the past ten years or so while working as a sales associate for Neiman Marcus. The finish on the metal handle was worn from the countless times she'd touched it. She reached for it one last time and entered the combination to unlock the door. When she swung it open, a decade of memories washed over her.

She removed a curled photo of herself on her first day of training—she looked young and eager, but behind the gap-toothed smile her dark eyes were troubled. Carlotta remembered how scared and panicked she'd been at that time, reeling in the wake of her parents' disappearance and wondering how she was going to feed and parent Wesley, while her own plans for the future had disintegrated. Until that time she'd led a pampered life, the only daughter of Randolph and Valerie Wren and accustomed to the best of everything—private schools, a lavish home, and guaranteed entry to the top tier of Buckhead society open only to the most exclusive families in Atlanta. All the things she'd taken for granted had been gone in a flash, and in the space of a few weeks, she'd morphed from a spoiled high school senior to a scared young woman in the workforce.

Swamped with nostalgia, she took down pictures of coworkers who had come and gone: Jolie Goodman, whom she and Hannah had initiated into party crashing during her short stint in the shoe department. Michael Lane, a friend whose mental illness and betrayal still haunted her. Patricia Alexander, who had started out

1

as a pesky hanger-on and wound up being Carlotta's choice for a personal assistant when she'd been promoted to director of the planned Atlanta bridal salon.

A lump of emotion swelled in her throat. Patricia had died under suspicious circumstances in her hotel bathroom when the two of them had traveled to Dallas to visit the flagship salon to learn the ropes. In the weeks that followed, Carlotta had clung to the belief that Patricia's death wasn't an accident, but she'd failed to convince anyone else, including the Dallas police and Detective Jack Terry. Even Cooper Craft, who normally gave her hunches the benefit of the doubt, had implored with her to accept the fact that Patricia's death was simply a tragic accident and get on with her life.

Carlotta bit into her lip. Maybe everyone else was right... maybe she was letting her guilt get the best of her—she still nursed pangs when she remembered the look on Patricia's face when she'd seen the unkind text messages Carlotta had exchanged with Hannah about Patricia's quirks. She'd accused Carlotta of offering her the position as her administrative assistant for the opportunity to punish her for admitting she'd taken a job with Neiman's at the behest of the District Attorney to spy on Carlotta and determine if she knew where her fugitive father was hiding out. But Carlotta hadn't begrudged Patricia—her parents had lost everything in the Ponzi scheme perpetrated by the investment firm where Randolph had worked.

Patricia had been looking out for her family, and who could blame her for that?

In truth, Carlotta admired Patricia's moxie. So the least she owed the woman was to find out if the used condom she'd found in her bathroom could lead back to a man who might've killed her.

"Carlotta, I thought that was you."

She turned to see Lindy Russell, the general manager of the Buckhead store and her longtime tough-love supporter. "Hi, Lindy. I'm just clearing out my things."

Lindy pressed her lips together. "I'm so sorry the bridal salon was cancelled. I hope you know I'd change it if I could."

"I do," she assured her former boss. The brick and mortar retail landscape wasn't looking so rosy these days.

"I wish you would reconsider staying on. You've been part of our sales family for so long."

She half-turned to transfer items from her locker to a cardboard box—makeup, snack bars, magazines and self-help books she'd meant to read. "All of my adult life."

"I know Patricia's death has affected you," Lindy murmured. "If you need to take some time off and come back when you're ready, I would understand."

Patricia's unexpected compliment when they were in Dallas came back to her. *I think you could do whatever you set your mind to.* Carlotta scraped the rest of the contents into the box in one motion, then turned.

"You're right," she offered. "Patricia's death has affected me, but not in the way you might think." She closed the empty locker and extended a smile to Lindy. "And I appreciate the offer, but it's time for me to move on."

"Ah… so you've already accepted another position?"

Carlotta was tempted to lie, but chickened out. "No. I'm not sure what my next step is yet, but I'll miss this place… and the people."

Lindy nodded, then stepped forward to give Carlotta's shoulders a squeeze. "Don't be a stranger."

Carlotta blinked in surprise at the gesture of affection. "O… kay."

"By the way, thanks for recommending that we bring on Quentin Gallagher."

The man she'd recommended to replace Patricia before the salon project had been scrapped. "So he's working out well?"

"I know he was hoping for a management position," Lindy said, "but he's already the number one sales associate in home decor, and he's sat in for my assistant twice when she was out sick. I think he'll move up quickly."

Carlotta smiled. "That's great."

Lindy angled her head. "You have a knack for seeing the best in people, Carlotta. I hope you find a way to make the most of it." She turned to leave.

"Lindy?"

"Yes?"

3

Carlotta gestured toward a locker on the end. "Has anyone cleared out Patricia's things?"

Lindy sighed. "No. I haven't had the heart."

"I'll do it."

"Would you?"

"Sure. I'm acquainted with her parents, I'll drop her things by their home."

Lindy stepped to the locker and removed a ring of keys from her belt. She found what Carlotta assumed was a master key to bypass the combination lock, then inserted it and opened the locker door. "Thanks for doing this, Carlotta."

"No problem."

Carlotta watched as her former boss walked away and took a call on her phone, already consumed with another work issue. Employees came and went, Carlotta knew, and she didn't expect any fanfare at her departure, especially since she'd quit in a blaze of glory after Lindy had told her plans for the bridal salon that she'd put countless hours toward were being ditched by corporate.

She stepped to Patricia's locker and withstood a pang of guilt to be snooping into her personal things. She removed a folded shopping bag and began to fill it with things the woman Hannah had dubbed "Country Club Barbie" had stashed inside: photos, makeup kit, hairspray, tampons, umbrella, and a myriad of other things. Carlotta tried not to focus on each item, just hurriedly transferred them to the shopping bag, then surveyed the empty locker with a sigh and closed the door.

After hefting the bag to her shoulder, she repositioned the cardboard box of her own things and headed toward the exit. When nostalgia washed over her, she decided to go the long way and thread through the women's departments, all of which she'd worked in at one time or another during her tenure at Neiman's.

She walked through racks and past tables of exquisite clothing, all of it merchandised beautifully and expertly, as was the Neiman's way. Well-heeled customers came to them for a luxurious experience of buying quality clothing in an exclusive environment, and she would miss the rarified air—not to mention the employee discount.

She sniffed back sudden tears—she'd be shopping the clearance racks into the foreseeable future.

As she made her way through the lingerie section, she spotted a familiar face just a few feet away. Tracey Tully Lowenstein—Carlotta's nemesis since high school—was holding up a lacy pink romper in front of her, gauging its fit. Carlotta's feet faltered, but before she could pivot, Tracey glanced up and noticed her. Her attractive face rearranged into a smirk, and she lowered the garment.

"Hello, Carlotta."

She'd last seen Tracey at a country club gala—Randolph had been making his triumphant return to society with Carlotta on his arm, and Tracey had been smarting over the reversal of fortunes as her father Walt Tully, Randolph's former friend and business partner, was on the run from federal charges of fraud and counterfeiting. Drunk and tearful, she'd confronted Carlotta in the women's restroom and said some nasty things.

Carlotta made her feet move forward. Once under the influence of painkillers she'd made a fantastical trip to an alternate universe where she'd learned what her life would've been like if her parents hadn't abandoned her and Wes. In that place, she and Tracey had been best friends, which wasn't a stretch considering they'd once moved in the same circles. She reminded herself now that if things had been different, she and Tracey would be as close as she was with Hannah.

Plus no matter how Tracey had treated her when they were young, she could afford to be gracious to the woman, especially since her own family was now intact.

Well... except for the little detail of Randolph not being her biological father.

"Hi, Tracey. How are you?"

Tracey's mouth twitched downward. "You mean how am I holding up with my father on the GBI's most-wanted list?" She laughed harshly, then held up the slinky garment. "I'm practicing retail therapy."

Carlotta offered her a little smile. "That's a good color for you."

She rehung the romper with a clatter of hangers. "Freddy doesn't like me in pink."

At the mention of the woman's smarmy gynecologist husband, Carlotta squashed the commentary in her head.

Tracey nodded to the box Carlotta held. "Did you get fired?"

"No... I quit."

Tracey's eyes widened. "Really? You've worked here so long, you practically blend in with the mannequins." She laughed at her own joke.

Carlotta kept smiling.

Tracey cocked her head. "I guess you can afford not to work since Randolph is back and flashing cash all around town. He bought a big new house and a golf course, I heard."

"A driving range," Carlotta corrected. "And I plan to work."

Tracey made a disgusted noise. "Don't tell me you're still moving bodies for the morgue."

Carlotta lifted her shoulder in a shrug. "Occasionally. I haven't had much time for it lately, but I won't rule it out."

"And rumor has it you're seeing an undertaker?"

"Dr. Cooper Craft," Carlotta confirmed. "And yes, he's the medical examiner at the morgue."

Tracey shuddered. "Jesus, Carlotta. I know Peter's in jail, but even conjugal visits would be better than sleeping with a mortician."

Carlotta tasted brine from the salty words she swallowed. "Peter and I are still friends, but only friends."

"He must feel so betrayed."

Carlotta inhaled, then exhaled. "I'm sure Peter realizes he put his trust in the wrong people, yes." Especially Walt Tully and Ray Mashburn, principals of Mashburn & Tully where he'd worked.

"He must be so lonely in that awful place," Tracey said, funneling the guilt back to Carlotta. "I understand why my dad would do anything not to be there."

Carlotta decided now wasn't the best time to say when Walt was eventually apprehended, his jailtime would likely be exponential what it might've been otherwise. "I should be going. Take care, Tracey." She turned to reroute around the lingerie department.

"Carlotta?"

She winced, then turned back.

Tracey held up the lacy romper, then offered a mean little smile. "Are you sure you don't want one last commission for old times' sake?"

Heat flooded Carlotta's face. How many times had Tracey and Angela Ashford and their cronies come into Neiman's and run her ragged to serve them with the carrot of a commission she desperately needed to pay the bills? She counted to five, then manufactured a smile. "I would, but Freddy doesn't like you in pink."

Carlotta stood long enough to see Tracey's mouth tighten, then turned and headed toward the exit, head held high.

Plus ten points.

CHAPTER 2

WESLEY WREN glanced around the shabby waiting room at the Midtown police precinct and realized with a start it was his first time on this side of the reception desk. How many times had Carlotta sat here, waiting for some word on his lame teenage ass?

He reached down self-consciously to yank his pants hem down over the thick black ankle monitor that marked him as a delinquent. His probation officer E. Jones said it would be removed soon, but for now it felt like an anvil.

Wes lifted his hand to find a piece of nail to chew on, then grimaced when a sharp bitter taste flooded his tongue. Cursing, he wiped his mouth on his sleeve, disgusted with himself. A grown man shouldn't have to resort to using a foul-tasting hand sanitizer to stop biting his nails. His father had even chastised him, told him card players should have nice hands and to knock it off.

Easier said than done. And he was learning that trying to stop a nervous habit on the heels of learning Meg Vincent, the lust and love of his life, had gone missing from her backpacking trip across Europe was a huge shitbag of a bad idea.

He lifted his hand for a gnaw and got another mouthful of nastiness. "Fuck!"

"Hey!"

He turned his head to see the woman at the window glaring at him.

"Do you kiss your sister Carlotta with that dirty mouth?"

Her nameplate read Brooklyn Berry. "You know Carlotta?"

"Sure do. How is she? Haven't seen her around here in a while."

He smirked. "That's because she and Detective Big Dick called it quits."

"Language," she warned with a pointed look. Then she leaned over the counter and lowered her chin. "No wonder Detective Terry's been in a worse mood than usual."

The side door opened and Jack Terry stood there, legs wide. "My ears are burning."

Wes never thought he'd be happy to see the man. He pushed to his feet. "I need to talk to you."

Jack blanched. "Is Carlotta okay?"

"Yeah, because you're out of her life."

The man frowned, but held the door while Wes walked through it. "What's this about?"

"Meg Vincent."

"Vincent... the local girl reported missing in Ireland?"

"Yeah."

"You know her?"

Wes lifted his fingers for a nibble, then grimaced at the taste and dropped his hand. "She's my, uh..."

"Girlfriend?"

He nodded. "I guess so."

"You don't know?"

Wes frowned. "*You're* giving relationship advice?"

Jack frowned back, then checked his watch. "Her parents are supposed to be here in a few minutes."

"I'm meeting them here. I'm early."

Jack closed the door, then asked Brooklyn to show the Vincents to his office when they arrived.

"Will do."

Wes followed Jack through a maze of cubicles. "I thought you were homicide. How'd you catch this case?"

"New position. I'm liaising with the GBI on some cases. Since this is international, it landed on my desk."

Wes followed him into an office—a big office—with a view. "Wow, that was some promotion."

Jack gave him a flat smile. "I guess someone thought Detective

Big Dick deserved a big office."

"You heard that, huh?"

"Yup."

Wes gestured to Jack's boring, dated clothing. "If you got a raise you should consider upping your wardrobe a notch."

Jack frowned. "*You're* giving fashion advice?"

"You look like hell, dude."

"Right back at you."

Wes lifted his hand, got a vile mouthful, then jerked it away. "I haven't slept much since I found out Meg is missing."

"That's understandable," Jack said, surprising him. He dropped into the chair behind his desk, gestured for Wes to sit, then pulled out a pad of paper. "So how long have you known this girl?"

"She's a woman."

"Okay. How long?"

"I met her when I worked at ASS."

"Ass?"

"Atlanta Systems Services, where I did my community service after you arrested me." He let that jab land before he continued. "She's a Georgia Tech student and was doing a work study there."

"Georgia Tech, huh?"

Wes smiled. "Yeah, she's a brainiac."

Jack grinned. "So why's she dating you?"

"That's hilarious." Although hadn't he asked himself that at least a hundred times?

A knock sounded on the door.

"Come in," Jack called.

The door opened to reveal Brooklyn. "The Vincents are here." She opened the door wider to allow Meg's parents inside. Dr. Harold Vincent and Ann Vincent looked worried and pale. Wes guessed they, too, hadn't slept. Mark, the friend of Meg's dead brother who was also in love with Meg, followed them inside. From the way his hand hovered at the waist of Meg's mother, it appeared he'd been helping them deal with this difficult situation. For the time being, Wes was willing to put aside his intense dislike of the guy, for Meg's sake. He had, after all, reached out to let Wes know she was missing. After not hearing from her for more than a week, he thought she'd lost interest in him. Now he only wished that was the case. He could live with Meg dumping him, but he couldn't live with—

"Wes," Jack said, pulling him out of his thoughts. "Are you with us?"

Everyone was staring at him. Worse, his eyes were full of unshed tears. He swiped at them. "Yeah." Then he stood and extended his hand to Meg's father. "Good to see you, sir."

Dr. Vincent let him stand with his hand out for a full five seconds.

Jack coughed. "Not under these circumstances, of course."

"Right," Wes added.

The man grudgingly shook his hand. Harold Vincent didn't like him, didn't think Wes was good enough for Meg, was probably rooting for Mark and his tennis sweaters.

Wes squeezed Ann's hand, then he and Mark exchanged nods, although Mark looked as if he'd rather head-butt him.

Jack introduced himself and explained his new role, then gestured to extra chairs. "Please, sit. Wes was telling me how he met Meg."

"You and Wesley are acquainted?" Dr. Vincent asked suspiciously.

"Yes," Jack said pleasantly. "I'm acquainted with everyone in Wes's family."

At least he hadn't thrown him under the bus, Wes conceded.

"If you don't mind," Jack said, "start at the beginning, tell me why your daughter went to Europe and as much you can remember about the people she traveled with. The more details, the better."

The Vincents had come prepared with photos of Meg and her planned itinerary for the summer. "Of course it was subject to change," her mother offered. "But Meg is responsible and careful, so we didn't worry as long as we heard from her regularly."

"How often was that?"

"About every other day. We printed out her text messages and the pictures she sent." They handed the pages to Jack, who scanned them, then made notes on the pad.

"And she was in touch with you, too, Wes?"

He nodded. "She texted at least once a day."

"Me, too," Mark said. "Meg texted me every single day."

Wes couldn't squash the barb of jealousy.

"Did you keep the texts?" Jack asked.

"Of course," Mark said, pointing to the file. "I printed them out."

Jack looked to Wes.

"I deleted them," he said morosely. Because he'd been angry and hurt when she'd stopped communicating.

"They must've meant a lot to you," Mark remarked.

"We can get them from her service provider if we need to," Jack intervened. "Do you remember when you last heard from her?"

"Nine days ago," Wes said, glaring at Mark.

"Same," Mark said, glaring back, and her parents nodded.

"And did she seem normal?"

"Yes," Mark and the Vincents chorused.

Jack looked back to Wes.

"Yeah. Except..."

"Except what?"

Wes shifted. "There was a guy in the group she was with. Meg didn't say, but I got the feeling from his body language in the pictures that he was kind of... into her."

That got everyone's attention.

"Do you know this guy's name?" her father asked in an anxious voice.

"No, she never said. And... I deleted the pictures."

"Great," Mark said, throwing up his hands.

Jack extended the sheet of pictures she'd texted to Mark and to her parents. "Wes, is he in any of these photos?"

Wes studied each one, then shook his head. "I don't think so. He had a man-bun, and was kind of stocky."

"Okay." Jack made more notes. "Dr. and Mrs. Vincent, who contacted you to tell you Meg was missing?"

"Two young women who were traveling with her, their names are on the sheet, along with the phone number the call came from. They were French, I believe, and only one of them spoke English. They were biking through Ireland. They said at first they thought Meg had left with a smaller group that had split off, but when they met up with the group again, those people hadn't seen Meg." The woman's voice ended on a sob and her husband patted her hand.

Wes looked away to keep from losing it in front of them. He raised his hand to chew and was rewarded with a nasty blast of the bitter chemical. "Ugh!"

They all looked at him.

"Sorry," he muttered, then stuffed his hands in his pockets.

Jack turned back to the Vincents. "And did the women you spoke to tell you when and where the group had split off?"

"They think it was the day after we last heard from her, and the town was Drogheda. They met up again in Dublin, and that's when they missed Meg." He pointed to where he'd marked it on the map.

"Do you know if they checked local hospitals?"

"They said they did, and hostels and other places. When they were looking for her, they saw a bracelet she wore in the window of a pawn shop in Lucan, here."

"And they knew the bracelet was Meg's?"

"Yes." Dr. Vincent cleared his throat. "Apparently, she was quite fond of the piece and they said she wouldn't have sold it." He pointed to a picture of the bracelet the friend had taken at the pawn shop.

"I gave her the bracelet," Wes blurted, proud to have something to add.

Jack raised an eyebrow. "You did?"

"Yeah," Wes said, irritated. "Girls like that stuff."

Suddenly Jack looked irritated too. Then he slid the photo toward Wes. "This is the same bracelet you gave her?"

Wes nodded. "The jeweler I bought it from said it was a custom piece."

Jack's other eyebrow went up, then he turned to Dr. Vincent. "They were smart to get a picture of the pawn shop sign. Have you been in touch with the local police in Lucan?"

"Yes," the man said in a choked voice, "but we didn't get anywhere."

"The GBI will be reaching out as well," Jack said. "And working with the embassy in Dublin. Dr. and Mrs. Vincent, what's the best way to reach you?"

"Here's my mobile number," Meg's mother said, reaching for the notepad to write it down.

"I'll be in Ireland," Dr. Vincent said, pushing to his feet.

"Sir," Jack said in a temperate voice, "I know you're concerned, but you really should leave this matter to the police."

"She's my little girl, and I'm going. Mark's going with me."

Mark stood close to Harold to show solidarity.

"Okay," Jack said with resignation. "Let me know when you land and where you're staying."

Wes popped up from his seat. "I want to go."

Dr. Vincent gave him a haughty look. "That's not a good idea."

"Wes," Jack said, then shook his head slightly to indicate "no."

"But I can help," Wes insisted. "I'll be one more person looking for her!"

Dr. Vincent crossed his arms, then nodded to the floor. "And how do you expect to get through security and customs with an ankle monitor?"

Wes's shoulders fell. Jack averted his gaze—he'd been trying to stop him from making a fool of himself.

"It's supposed to come off soon," Wes mumbled, but nobody cared.

"Let's go, Ann," Dr. Vincent said, then helped his wife to her feet.

"I'll show you out," Jack said, then looked at Wes and mouthed, "Stay."

Wes frowned. As if he was a dog.

He watched them walk away, a cozy little trio united in their anguish over Meg, and felt like an outsider, as if he wasn't good enough to love her. Frustration welled in his chest. He lifted his hand for a comforting nibble, and when the bitter taste hit his tongue, he ignored it and sucked the offending coating off the ends of his fingers—both hands.

"Wes?"

He stopped and looked up to find Jack staring at him, looking concerned. "Are you alright?"

Wes removed his slobbery fingers from his mouth and wiped them on his pants leg. "I'm fine. Why did you want me to stay?"

"Mostly to spare you from Dr. Vincent."

"He's always hated me."

"Don't take it personally. When victim's relatives are upset, they need to take it out on someone."

Wes blinked. "You think Meg is a victim?"

Jack lifted his hand. "Bad choice of words. For all we know, she could've gotten lost and she's safe in a place where she doesn't have cell phone service."

"What about her bracelet?"

Jack grunted. "Let's hope she got mad at you for some reason and sold it. Or maybe it fell off her arm and someone found it."

Because of the bracelet's intricate closure Wes didn't think so, but he realized Jack was trying to be optimistic. "I should go to Ireland with them."

"Do you have a passport?"

Wes sagged. "No... but I can get one."

"Not until your attorney settles the Vegas charges and that ankle monitor is removed." Jack clasped his shoulder. "Why don't you lie low and let Dr. Vincent be the hero here?"

"And Marky Mark?" Wes groused.

"Yeah. If she cares about you, when it's all over, she'll be coming home to you."

Wes jerked away from him and walked to the office door. "Is that what you tell yourself about Carlotta?"

A muscle worked in Jack's jaw. "I'll let you know if I hear anything about Meg."

Wes nodded, then turned and walked out.

CHAPTER 3

"AND HOW did it feel to quit your job?"

Carlotta sat in a chair facing her psychologist Dr. Denton. On the heels of her parents' bombshell that Randolph Wren wasn't her biological father, she'd sought out professional help to sort through years of suppressed emotions. And after a rocky beginning, she was warming up to confiding in the gently rumpled older man. An involuntary smile pulled at her mouth. "At the moment, it was... exhilarating. I felt as if a world of opportunities had opened to me."

He nodded his graying head. "And now?"

She crossed her leg at the knee, registering a flash of pleasure at the sight of her Golden Goose fuchsia booties, then sighed. "Now I feel as if a world of opportunities has opened to me... and I don't know what to do next."

"Do you have regrets about leaving?"

She worked her mouth back and forth. "Sometimes. I was good at my job."

"Why?"

"Pardon me?"

"Why were you good at your job?"

She gave a little shrug. "Because I've been doing it for a long time."

He nodded. "So don't you think you'll be good at something else if you give it time?"

"I… suppose. I'm just afraid I'll make the wrong decision."

"What might be the result of a wrong decision?"

"Embarrassment… failure… heartbreak."

One of his eyebrows twitched. "Heartbreak? That's an unusual emotion to assign to a wrong career move."

She shifted in the chair. "I misspoke."

"Did you?"

She nodded. "I'm just overwhelmed with choices, especially since I'm not qualified to do very many things."

"Why do you say that?"

"Because I didn't go to college."

"And you think a college degree is important?"

"Society does… and yes, I guess I do, too. It's a sign of accomplishment."

"You could go to college now," he suggested mildly.

Her pulse ticked up. "I'm too old."

"That's not true. I didn't finish my degree until I was in my forties. Lots of people go to college when they're adults. By then they have a better idea of what they want to study, and they tend to take it more seriously."

"Wes inherited the smart genes."

"I see. And what did you inherit?"

She gave a little laugh. "Apparently my mother's questionable taste in men."

"Ah. We're back to heartbreak."

Carlotta frowned. "No. It was a joke."

He smiled. "Okay." He glanced up at the clock. "Our time is up. Can I give you something to think about?"

Although she was pretty sure she didn't want the homework, she nodded.

"Over the next few days, I'd like for you to question your limiting beliefs."

"What do you mean?"

"I mean you seem to have a set of beliefs about what you can and can't do. Write down some of those absolutes… then question them."

"O… kay. How will that change anything?"

The shoulders of his worn corduroy sport coat lifted with his shrug. "It might not change anything at all. But will you humor me?"

She stood, then reached for her bag. "Okay, I'll do it."

He stood and accompanied her to the door of his office.

"Dr. Denton, how is George?" The unstable patient who'd pretended to be the doctor at Carlotta's first appointment. She'd spilled her guts to him before the real Dr. Denton had arrived.

The man made a rueful noise. "I don't discuss my patients."

She gave him a pointed look.

"But in this case I'll make an exception," he continued. "George is struggling. He continues to take on personalities of other people. But in time I'm hopeful he'll come to realize his own value."

"I hope so, too," she said, and meant it.

As she made her way out of the building, she fingered the locket at her throat. Inside was the black and white photo of her unknown father. She'd shown it to George when she'd thought he was a therapist, and he'd said the face looked familiar.

And Patricia had said the same thing. Was it possible her father was a public figure, a celebrity of some kind?

She longed to talk to Hannah about it, but she hadn't yet told her friend her earthshaking news. In fact, other than Dr. Denton and George, the only people who knew were her parents and Wes...

And Jack.

She closed her eyes briefly... Jack Terry seemed to have his finger—or another body part—in whatever problem she happened to be facing. But she'd finally come to the realization that he'd never be able to offer what she needed, and it had allowed her to see Coop in a new light. They were taking things slowly, flirting and dating, and easing into what she hoped would become a deeper, more emotional bond.

As she headed to the nearest train station, her phone vibrated with a text. When she saw it was from Coop, her heart sprang up.

Scored another part for the Miata, can I come over?

He was fixing up the white convertible Randolph had given her when she turned sixteen. Selling it, she'd decided, would be a cathartic way to break with the past.

Come on over... getting on the train, see you in a few.

She stowed the phone, then hurried down the station steps to catch the next train to Lindbergh. The car was crowded and she realized she'd lost track of time, and everyone who was still gainfully employed was getting off work. She glanced from somber face to somber face, tempted to ask each passenger what they did for a living so she could strike it off her list.

Would she turn into a nine-to-five zombie, too?

At the Lindbergh stop, she exited with a crush of people, then turned on the sidewalk toward the townhouse she shared with Wes. Her heart squeezed for her little brother—his beloved Meg had gone missing on a backpack trip across Europe. He'd already been heartsick from missing her, and now came this worrisome news. She prayed the girl was simply off on a side adventure... but she'd seen the darker side of people, and the pretty blond American might've been an easy target for someone with criminal motives.

A few feet ahead she spotted the co-working space where she'd had the DNA kits sent that she'd ordered anonymously; according to the tracking number, the package had been delivered. And since the place looked to be hopping because of rush hour, she decided it would be a good time to claim it. As she approached the entrance she noted the names of the space's bigger clients mounted next to the door: Molten & Poole, IndieWick, Roberson Consulting. She hung back until a woman approached the door juggling a briefcase and coffee with her magnetic key card extended, then rushed forward to arrive at the same time. She smiled at the women and when the click sounded, said, "Let me get that for you." She opened the door and the woman thanked her, then said, "Oh, I love your booties!"

"Thanks," Carlotta said, beaming. She followed the woman inside, then peeled off to the reception desk.

"May I help you?" a young man asked.

"I hope so," she said earnestly. "My supervisor sent me to pick up a package."

"It should be in your company mailbox," he said, gesturing to an adjacent wall of locked cabinets. "It'll match the number on your key card."

She winced. "I checked, but it's not there, although the tracking number says it was delivered."

He frowned. "What company do you work for?"

"Roberson Consulting, but the package should also have the

name Pat Johnson." The fake name she'd used to order the kits.

He looked under the counter, then pulled out a small package. "Pat Johnson—here it is. They left off the company name."

Her shoulders dropped in relief. "Thank you, you *saved* me."

He grinned. "No problem." Then he winked. "I'll see you around."

"Okay," she said happily, then turned and made a circuitous path to the exit.

Outside she exhaled, then opened the package to remove the instructions and scanned them as she walked toward the townhome. It was the only kit on the market that allowed customers to submit semen for genetic testing... but she worried the sample she'd removed from Patricia's hotel room would be too dated to test. From what she could tell through the plastic baggie, the contents of the condom were the consistency of dried cake icing.

She found the section on preparing the sample and winced—it had to be liquid enough for a cotton swab to absorb.

Her disappointment was acute.

The temperature had bumped higher, and traffic on the streets was thick and impatient. She hadn't missed having a car since she'd turned in the rental, but if her next job wasn't on the train line, she'd have to buy one with the proceeds of the Miata.

Randolph had offered to buy her a BMW, but now it seemed like a price for her silence... and her forgiveness.

She pushed the troubling thoughts from her mind and hurried the last block home. When she walked up the driveway to the townhouse, though, she fought a frown—their neighbor Mrs. Winningham was standing at the fence, holding her unfortunate-looking dog Toofers.

"Carlotta!"

"Hi, Mrs. Winningham."

The nosy woman leaned over the chest-high fence. "The man driving that van is in your garage."

"I know. Thank you."

"What's he doing in there?"

"He's fixing my car."

"Is he a boyfriend of yours?"

Carlotta hesitated, then smiled. "He's not *a* boyfriend, he's *the* boyfriend."

The woman sniffed. "What happened to the cowboy?"

Carlotta frowned. "He had his chance, and he blew it."

"So this guy is the consolation prize?"

She pushed her tongue into her cheek. "Goodbye, Mrs. Winningham."

"We have a neighborhood ordinance against working on clunker cars!" Toofer added his two cents with a bevy of snarls.

Carlotta ignored them and walked to the garage. The door was up and blues music sounded from inside. The nice-looking lower half of Cooper Craft stuck out from underneath the raised hood of the Miata. He was shirtless and sweaty and sexy as hell. Carlotta stood and admired the view until he straightened and noticed her. He grinned. "Hey, you."

She grinned. "Hey, you." She walked up for a kiss, but he held up his hands.

"I'm all sweaty."

Carlotta admired his muscled chest and arms. "And it looks good on you."

Coop laughed, then leaned forward for a no-hands kiss. His mouth was warm and welcoming and just so... wonderful. Her body responded with tingling anticipation that sometime soon they would know each other's bodies intimately.

When he pulled back, his dark eyes were smoldering. "It's getting harder and harder to resist you."

Her chest filled with feminine satisfaction. "That's the plan."

He groaned. "I'll never get this car working if you keep distracting me."

She laughed, then surveyed the exposed motor. "How's it going?"

"Slowly... won't be able to fire it up until I find a couple more pieces, but I have feelers out all over."

"I can't tell you how much I appreciate this, Coop."

"You know I'm glad to help you any way I can."

She bit into her lip. "Really?"

His brow furrowed. "Uh-oh. What did I just volunteer for?"

She inhaled. "Can you tell me how to rehydrate semen for a DNA test?"

His eyes bounced wide. "Come again?" Then he shook his

head. "Scratch that. *Why* do you need to know?" He glanced at her stomach. "Are you—?"

"No! Of course not. Besides, how could I be?"

He smiled. "Just checking."

"It's for a friend." Not a lie. "She... was dating more than one guy and she needs to know which guy left a particular sample, but the sample isn't... fresh. I thought you might have a suggestion for how I—er, how *she* could bring it back to life, so to speak."

He looked dubious, then sighed and scratched his head. "In the lab I'd use serum, but a drop or two of good quality distilled water would do in a pinch."

Her hopes buoyed. "Great!" Then she sobered. "I mean—good to know. Thank you."

He still looked unconvinced. "You're welcome... I think. Quick—kiss me before I think about this too much."

She laughed and leaned in for another really, really good kiss. "Umm," she murmured. "Stay for dinner?"

He wrinkled his nose. "Are you cooking?"

She gave him a playful swat. "Why would I cook when you and Wes are so good at it?"

He laughed and nuzzled her neck, sending chills over her shoulders. "So you only love me for my culinary skills?"

Carlotta froze.

Coop pulled back. "I didn't mean... I was kidding."

Her mouth opened to reassure him, but her vital signs had spiked and short-circuited her brain. Love?

A noise from the driveway caught their attention. Wes appeared on his bike, jumping off before it came to a stop. "Hey."

She was grateful for the timely interruption. "Hey."

"Hi, Wes," Coop offered.

"Any word on Meg?" she asked.

Wes gave a short head shake devoid of emotion, meaning, of course, he was worried sick. "I picked up shrimp for dinner. You two wanna help me peel?"

She and Coop exchanged anguished looks as Wes stowed his bike.

"Sure," Coop said, reaching for his shirt.

"Absolutely," Carlotta said.

She and Wes both always seemed to be off balance in the romance department.

CHAPTER 4

"HANNAH, OPEN up!" Carlotta pounded on the door of Hannah Kizer's apartment. She juggled a box of pastries and two coffees, and her arms were about to give out.

The scrape of the deadbolt sounded, then the chained door opened six inches to reveal Hannah's face, fully made up with scarlet lipstick and false eyelashes. "You're early."

"So? Neither one of us is employed at the moment."

"I'm... occupied."

A spicy scent floated out into the hall. "Yum, are you cooking?"

"No." Hannah's perfect pout twitched. "Maybe. Give me a few minutes."

"Wait—" She was cut off by the door slamming shut.

She sighed, then reasoned maybe Hannah's husband Chance Hollander had swung by for a quickie. They were an odd couple who still maintained separate residences until Hannah could break the news to her monied family that she'd married a chubby pothead who trafficked prescription drugs, porn, and had allegedly slept with every prostitute walking the legendary corridor of Ponce de Leon Avenue.

Although, she conceded as she lowered herself to the floor and opened the box of pastries, the guy did seem completely head over heels for Hannah.

She rummaged through the selections, then took a healthy bite out of an unhealthy éclair.

And honestly, who was she to judge compatibility? Coop's inadvertent drop of the "L" word the previous evening still had her flustered. Coop was eminently lovable—he was handsome and kind and sexy. He'd been a mentor and friend to Wes, and he'd been instrumental in uncovering her mother's dementia misdiagnosis. He was well regarded among his coworkers at the morgue, and had bent the rules more than once to indulge her pursuit of justice when evidence in a death pointed elsewhere. And he'd always been there for her when she needed someone to lean on.

What was not to love?

She took another big gooey bite and chewed resolutely, turning her mind away from the uncomfortable conversation to the matter at hand. She'd decided to tell Hannah about the circumstances of her birth and to get her help with the DNA kits. She needed to confide in someone before she flew apart.

So why hadn't she told Coop?

Suddenly the door swung open and Hannah stuck her head out. "Okay, you can come in."

Carlotta handed her the box of pastries and pushed to her feet. "The coffee's probably cold," she groused.

"We'll nuke it."

She followed her friend through the door into her vintage high-ceilinged, open plan apartment, then squinted at her outfit— black leather corset, tap pants and a blood-red silk kimono. "Is Chance here?"

"No. He's at your dad's driving range every waking hour. He fucking loves that place."

Carlotta smirked. "Unlike Wes, much to Randolph's dismay."

"Yeah, I gathered as much. Hey, I heard Wes's girlfriend disappeared or some shit in Ireland?"

"That's as much as I know. He's not talking about it, but I know he's upset." She gestured in a figure-eight to Hannah's outfit. "What's this all about?"

"This? Oh… like you said, I've been cooking." She nodded toward the kitchen where the counters and sinks were littered with dirty pots and pans.

Carlotta raised an eyebrow. "Since when do you dress up like Bettie Page to cook?"

Hannah gave a little wave. "Sometimes the mood to cook just strikes out of the blue, you know what I mean?"

"Not even a little bit. I can't cook, remember?"

"Sure you can. You've just never had to."

"Or wanted to." She shook her head. "It boggles my mind that you actually pay money to go to culinary school."

"Actually, that would be my father's money, as he so often reminds me. And I still don't have a diploma, which he also often reminds me."

"Have you decided if you're going back?"

Hannah made a face. "I'm half afraid if I finish, my dad will want me to be a chef in one of his hotel restaurants."

"And if you don't finish?"

"My dad will want me to *manage* one of his hotel restaurants."

"Ah. And do you have a preference?"

"Yes—not working for my dad."

She shrugged. "Then don't—figure out something else to do."

A sly look came over Hannah's face. "I'm working on it."

Carlotta smiled. "What is it?"

"I'll tell you once I have the details worked out."

"Can you give me a hint?"

"Um… it's an online business."

"Sounds intriguing."

"You should think about doing something online, too."

Carlotta frowned. "Like what?"

"Anything—buy and sell those vintage designer clothes you like."

She gave a laugh. "I have zero technical skills—I can barely send an email, much less run an online business."

Hannah shrugged. "It was just a thought." She opened the box of pastries and sniffed.

"I bought one of those honey buns you like."

"Maybe later—I'm kind of full."

"What did you make?"

"A rack of barbecue ribs, a half-pound of thick cut sweet potato fries, and a loaf of garlic pull-apart bread."

"Mm," Carlotta said, moving toward the kitchen. "I'll have some." She opened the refrigerator and looked inside, but didn't see any containers among the jam-packed shelves.

"Uh—sorry... I ate it."

Carlotta closed the fridge door. "All of it?"

"Yeah."

"Jesus, no wonder you're full."

Hannah frowned. "Enough about me, what's this big secret project you wanted to tell me about?"

Suddenly nervous, Carlotta held up her nearly empty cup of coffee. "Do you mind if I use your bathroom first?"

"Knock yourself out."

She made her way to the bathroom, telling herself she still had time to change her mind. Once she told Hannah, the bell couldn't be unrung.

The door to Hannah's bedroom sat ajar and as she walked by she couldn't miss the tripod standing next to the bed... and the white backdrop on the opposite wall. Was Hannah's online business doing live porn?

Carlotta puffed out her cheeks, then proceeded on to the bathroom. She wouldn't put it past her eccentric friend to do something like that for fun... but for profit?

On the other hand, she thought wryly, who knew what she herself would be willing to do in a few weeks if she hadn't found a job?

When she emerged, Hannah had cleaned up the kitchen area, was arranging pans and utensils in the dishwasher. When she straightened, she belched loudly, then put her fist under her breastbone. "Ugh, sorry about that." She opened a cabinet door and removed a bottle of antacid, then popped a couple in her mouth.

"Are you okay?"

"Stress eating," Hannah said absently. "Now... what's the dealeo?"

Carlotta reached for her bag, then pulled out the two DNA kits and set them on the table.

Hannah shrieked. "I knew this day would come! You're pregnant, and you don't know if the father is Jack or Coop or Peter."

Carlotta frowned. "Not even close."

"Dammit." Hannah pulled out a chair and sat down. "What then?"

"Actually, it involves you."

"Christ, Carlotta, spill it."

She pulled out the opposite chair and sat. "Not you exactly, but your family's Dallas hotel."

Hannah sighed. "This has something to do with Patricia's death."

"Yes."

"It was ruled an accident. Let it go already."

"What if it wasn't an accident? What if instead of falling and hitting her head, someone was in her room that night and killed her?"

Hannah crossed her arms. "Where is this going, Carlotta?"

From a side compartment, she removed the sealed baggie that contained the used condom.

"Wait—I recognize that condom," Hannah said. "It was in one of the pictures you sent me from Dallas."

"Right. I found the baggie when I went back to Patricia's room after the body was removed."

"The condom was already in the baggie?"

"Yeah."

"That doesn't make sense."

"It was next to the trash can, so maybe she or the guy it belonged to dropped it in a baggie before tossing it just to keep from making a mess."

"So you think whoever left the condom might've killed her, but what does that have to do with the DNA kit?"

"Since the police won't reopen the case, I'm going to send off the sample to get a genetic profile, then I'll see if there are any hits on the global family tree that have the last name of one of the suspects."

"How many suspects do you have, Miss Marple?"

"Two. There's the guy from the dating app she was supposed to meet."

"Do you have his name?"

"John Smythe."

"You're joking, right?"

"I tried to warn Patricia she was being catfished, but it made her angry. Later she texted I was right, but didn't say how."

"But you don't know that John Smythe was in her room."

"There were leftovers from two room service meals in her room."

"Did the wait staff see anyone else when they delivered the meals?"

"They were questioned and said no, but the man could've been out of sight."

"Or she could've ordered two meals and eaten them both," Hannah said. "Especially if her date went south, I've done that plenty of times."

Carlotta nodded. "There was also a guy at the airport taxi stand, Trevor Biondi, who flirted with her. Patricia gave him her card, so he had her number and he knew where she was staying because he called the car for us. What if after the date with John Smythe went south, she hooked up with Trevor?"

"Could be, but that doesn't mean he killed her."

"Except get this—I tried to find him when I went back to the airport. A coworker said he'd quit his job and moved to the West Coast, just like that."

Hannah frowned. "Okay, that's suspicious."

"I know, right? I'll know more about who she might've talked to that night when I get her phone."

"I thought you said her phone was missing."

"It was... and then it was found. I asked the person at the hotel to ship it to me."

"Okay, that only broke ten kinds of protocol the staff should be following."

"I, um, might have suggested the phone was her work phone. The point is, if Patricia was in contact with the guy at the taxi stand and if this sample belongs to him, we at least have proof he was in her room."

Hannah leaned forward to peer at the baggie. "So you're going to submit this under his name?"

"No... anonymously. I bought it online and made sure the purchase can't be traced back to me. And I'll register the kit under a fake name and email address from a public computer."

She lifted a perfectly arched dark brow. "I thought you said you had zero technical skills?"

"I'm sure someone who knew what they were doing could've skipped a few steps."

"But you figured it out."

Carlotta pursed her mouth. "I guess I did."

"So is there anything distinctive about this Biondi guy that would tie him to the genetic profile?"

"He's African American."

"That narrows it down some."

"Unless John Smythe is also," Carlotta pointed out.

Hannah pulled her hand down her face. "This seems like *such* a long shot."

"It is! Which is why the police would never do it. This plan—"

"I'd call it more of a *scheme*."

"—might go nowhere, but it's worth trying, don't you think?"

Hannah worked her mouth back and forth, then finally nodded. "It's worth trying."

Carlotta grinned. "I knew you'd agree."

"Let's do it before I change my mind. If this case gets reopened, my dad is going to be pissed. Do you know what it does to a hotel's rate when there's a murder on the property?"

"About that," Carlotta said. "Can you get the security footage from the hotel for the night Patricia died?"

Hannah gaped. "Do you know how many hoops I'd have to jump through for that?"

"So that's a yes?"

"Ugh! I'm not making any promises." She sighed. "What do we have to do to submit the sample?"

"Rehydrate the semen."

Hannah rolled her eyes upward. "I doubt we can learn how to do that on YouTube."

"We don't have to. Coop taught me."

Her friend made an orgasmic sound. "Of course he did. If you don't marry that man, I'm going to talk to him about being a throuple with me and Chance."

Carlotta laughed, then pulled a bottle of distilled water from her bag. "We need a sharp knife, tweezers, and an eye dropper."

Hannah left to gather the items, and when she returned to the table, Carlotta could tell she was warming up to the project. In fact, she insisted on wearing latex gloves and sterilizing a spoon to mix a sliver of the dried semen with two drops of distilled water herself.

"Swab," she said, holding out her hand.

Carlotta passed her the swab to soak up the tiny sample, then held the shipping vial while she carefully dropped it inside.

"How long will it take to get the results?" Hannah asked.

"About three weeks."

"Gotta love science." Then she spied the second DNA test. "Did you bring a spare in case we messed up the first one?"

Carlotta hesitated. "No."

"What then?"

She reached up to finger the locket around her neck. "Remember I told you mom gave me this necklace?"

"Right. You said it had a picture of your dad inside."

She nodded, then opened the locket to reveal the tiny black and white photo. "This was one of the gifts she left under the Christmas tree when they skipped town."

Hannah leaned forward. "Hm. That doesn't look like Randolph."

"That's because it isn't."

Her friend's eyes suddenly went wide. "You mean—?"

"They told me Randolph isn't my real father."

"Holy shit, Carlotta. How did you react?"

"I was hurt… and angry."

"Now I understand why things were awkward when we moved you out of their house."

Carlotta nodded. "Things are somewhat better now."

"Does Wes know?"

"He knows. But you're the only other person I've told. Oh, and Jack knows."

"You told Detective Dickhead?"

"No. Once when he was doing surveillance at the townhouse, he went behind my back and opened the gifts under the tree thinking he'd find a clue about where Randolph had gone."

"So he's known all this time?"

Carlotta nodded.

"Ugh, I hate him." Then Hannah frowned. "Wait—Valerie didn't tell you who your father is?"

"No. And I told them I didn't want to know."

"Oh."

Carlotta held up the extra DNA kit. "But I lied."

Hannah's mouth rounded in realization. *"Oh."*

STEPHANIE BOND

CHAPTER 5

"HAVE YOU gone to the local news people?" Wes shouted into the phone.

"Yeah," Mark said, sounding tired and irritated. "But no one seems to be taking this seriously, thinks Meg is a ditzy American girl who's off shopping."

"*Make* them take it seriously, dude. Isn't that why you went over there?"

A heavy sigh sounded. "I came over to make sure her dad isn't alone if he gets bad news."

Wes's intestines cramped. "You can't think the worst. Did you print up flyers with her picture on it? She might have amnesia."

"That's not how things are done around here. We have to work with the locals, and they want to wait."

"That's bullshit! If I was over there—"

"But you're not," Mark cut in. "So do me a favor, and stop calling like a psycho and grilling me. I told you I'd call when I have news, and I will."

"Don't—" But the asshole had already ended the call.

Wes pulled back his arm to hurl his phone.

"That won't help anything."

He stopped and looked up to see his dad had stepped inside the lobby of the Lindbergh Family Driving Range, and apparently had overheard the tail end of his conversation. Misery welled in his chest—not only did he feel helpless, but he was stuck in this place doing mindless tasks for mindless customers. To his horror, tears filled his eyes.

"Okay," Randolph said in a gentler voice. "Why don't you and I go hit a bucket of balls?"

"I don't want to," Wes said through gritted teeth.

"I know," Randolph said. "Do it anyway because you obviously feel like hitting something."

He didn't respond, but he didn't object when his dad pulled a bucket of balls from the counter where they were lined up and chose two drivers from their higher tiered rental rack. Feeling as if he might fly apart, he dragged his skinny ass after his dad, following him out onto the tee that was crowded for a weekday. Business was growing, he registered distantly... all due to his buddy Chance's improvements. Wes wished he cared half as much.

Randolph walked to the far end of the tee, probably, Wes surmised, so fewer people would witness his son's ineptitude with a club. Randolph handed him a driver, golf tee, and ball. "There you go. Hit the hell out of it."

The overhead sun was hot as fuck. The glare off his glasses practically blinded him, but his eye-hand coordination was so bad, it didn't really matter. He jammed the wooden tee into the short grass, then set the ball on top. Next to him Randolph was doing the same in his section of the tee, with his back to Wes. Knowing his dad wasn't watching him made him more fearless. He adopted a lax stance, then lifted and swung the club wildly, not giving two shits if it connected with the ball.

But it did.

The ball sailed crazily high, then fell at a respectable distance. Wes acknowledged a blip of satisfaction, then immediately wanted to smack the ball again.

In front of him, Randolph swung for a nice drive, then said over his shoulder, "So... what's the news from Ireland?"

"Nothing good," Wes mumbled while he teed up another shot. "Mark said the local police are being dicks, that they don't believe a crime has been committed."

Randolph swung again. "So they're not looking for her?"

Wes whacked the ball. "Nope."

"Is her father working with the embassy?"

"Allegedly, although Mark says the officials there are letting the local police take the lead."

Randolph swung again. "Do they have any clues to go on?"

Wes set down another ball, then stepped back to hack it hard. "The police talked to everyone in the group she was traveling with except the guy from the photos she sent that gave me the creeps."

"Why haven't the police talked to him?"

Wes took his time answering. He set another ball, then swung the club as if he were aiming at the man-bun guy's head. The ball exploded off the tee, arcing high and far—the best drive of his life. "He's disappeared too." Then he hacked at the ground. "Why did I delete those pictures?"

"Don't beat yourself up," Randolph said. "The police can get them from the phone service carrier."

"Yeah, but apparently that takes a while."

Randolph swung. "Surely some of the other people she was traveling with have a picture of the guy."

"If the police thought to ask before they all scattered," Wes said. He blinked back moisture and set another ball on the tee. "I need to go over there."

"No, you don't," Randolph said easily.

"Yes, I do," Wes ground out. "I left ten messages for the attorney you hired telling him I need to get this damn ankle monitor removed, and he hasn't called me back."

Randolph swung again, sending the ball on a beautiful trajectory. "Let Meg's father and the local police handle everything. This can't be the first time something like this has happened."

Wes sputtered. "Women don't just up and disappear. Something bad happened."

His father didn't speak, but his body language was stiff.

"What are you not saying?" Wes asked.

Randolph sighed, then turned to look at Wes. "She wouldn't be the first young woman to run away with some guy she met on vacation."

Wes set his jaw. "She didn't... she wouldn't."

"But if she did, you can see how your presence over there would make things even more awkward once she's found." Randolph stooped to set another ball, then smoothly swung for another beautiful shot.

Wes breathed in and out. The only thing that kept him from losing it were the words "once she's found." He didn't want to believe Meg had run off with the guy in the pictures, but he could live with it if it meant she was unharmed.

Even though the thought of it hurt like a gunshot.

CHAPTER 6

"Is THIS okay?" the Uber driver asked, pulling to a stop.

Carlotta glanced out the window at the imposing Fulton County Correctional Facility. "Yes, I can get out here. Thank you."

She exited the car and inhaled deeply to calm her unsettled stomach. Once upon a time, her world had revolved around the next time she would see Peter Ashford. Now it was a dreaded obligation. He hadn't been himself the last time she'd visited, had seemed paranoid. He'd rambled about Randolph having a secret that even Valerie didn't know about... but then strangely, had assured Carlotta that Randolph would protect her. She hoped Peter was in a clearer frame of mind today and she could determine if he actually knew something, or if the anxiety of being incarcerated had led to an emotional and cognitive break.

Eager to get the visit behind her, she walked briskly toward the entrance, then stopped when a familiar figure emerged. "Dad?"

The endearment had popped out before she could think about it. It was as if she'd conjured him up. Randolph turned his head in her direction and did a double-take.

"Carlotta?" His body language struck her as awkward, but by the time he reached her, he was smiling wide. He had aged well and was still so handsome. "Hello, Sweetheart. You look beautiful."

Reminding herself to make an effort, she thanked him, then gave him a hug. "What are you doing here?"

"I needed to talk to Wes's attorney and he was here."

"Is everything okay with Wes?"

"Yes. This was about having his ankle monitor removed."

"Oh, good."

"I assume you're visiting Peter?"

She nodded. "I don't know if it'll help him, but I feel like I should."

"It'll help him. Even though it isn't prison, this is a terrible place for someone like Peter."

"That's generous of you, considering the part he played at Mashburn & Tully."

"He was in over his head. I just wish he'd gotten out of there sooner."

Guilt stabbed her. Peter had once asked her to move to New York with him. If she had, both of their lives might've been so different.

"How are things around the townhouse?" Randolph asked.

"They're fine. The renovations look fantastic. And I assume you know that Wes turned your and Mom's old bedroom into a home office for me."

He nodded, then looked wistful. "That boy thinks the world of you."

"He thinks the world of you, too," she murmured. "He wants you to be proud of him."

"I am."

She angled her head. "You're a little hard on him."

"He needs guidance... I want him to be equipped to handle whatever life throws his way."

"I think he's already proved he can," she said lightly.

He pressed his mouth together, then nodded. "You both have."

Carlotta warmed under the unexpected praise.

"Your mother said you left Neiman Marcus?"

"I did. The bridal salon was scrapped, and my position along with it. I didn't want to go back to the sales floor, so I decided it was time to move on." She gave him a wry smile. "Move on to what, I don't yet know."

"You'll think of something. Besides, you deserve a break."

She appreciated his reference to the fact that she'd worked away her twenties to provide for herself and Wes. She gestured to the entrance of the jail. "I should go in."

"Right. Carlotta..." His expression turned somber. "Keep an eye out for anything odd around the townhouse. With Walt Tully in the wind... well, considering the way he feels about me, he might decide that retaliation against any Wren will do."

The thought slid into her mind that that would exclude her, but she didn't say it.

Although from the flash of pain in his eyes, he'd read her mind.

"I'm sure Mrs. Winningham will alert me if she sees anything amiss."

He gave a little laugh. "No doubt. Come by the new house soon. Your mom misses you... Prissy, too."

"I will," she promised.

He offered a fatherly smile, then lowered a quick kiss on her cheek. "Bye, Sweetheart."

She watched him walk away and was once again assailed with a stew of emotions. She wished she didn't know Randolph wasn't her biological father. She wished things could go back to the way they were a few weeks ago. After a decade apart, everything had finally been right with the Wren family... for all of about ten minutes.

Pushing aside useless regrets, she turned toward the entrance of the facility and hurried inside. She'd dressed in bright colors to counter the bleakness of the place. She made her way into the bowels of the building to the waiting room where she stood in line to access a kiosk and sign in. After more waiting, she was called to a window.

"You're Ms. Wren?" the uniformed man asked.

"Yes."

"And you're here to see Peter Ashford?"

"That's right."

"I'm sorry, ma'am, but he's not allowed visitors."

Carlotta frowned. "Is he sick? Has he been injured?"

"We're not allowed to share that information."

She wet her lips, then lowered her voice. "Look, I just want to know if he's okay."

He sighed, then leaned in. "He's okay. He and another inmate got into it and they're both being disciplined, that's all."

She exhaled. "For how long?"

"A week. The warden wants to keep him isolated until his bail hearing so he has the best shot. Dust-ups with other prisoners don't look good."

"That's nice of the warden."

"Ashford's a decent guy, he's been giving us guards investment advice."

Carlotta smiled. "That sounds like Peter. I know this is a lot to ask, but can you at least get word to him that I was here?"

The man scanned her face, then gave her a little wink and nodded.

She thanked him, then backtracked through the building, nursing an odd mixture of relief and disappointment she hadn't gotten to see Peter.

But acknowledging a surprising spike of pleasure at seeing her dad... er, Randolph.

CHAPTER 7

"RESIDENT'S NAME, please?" the gate attendant asked.

"Randolph and Valerie Wren," Carlotta said from the backseat of the Lyft car.

"And your name?"

"Carlotta Wren."

He stepped back into the guard shack at the entrance of the gated community, presumably to call and confirm her access, then reappeared with a smile. "Take the first right, then the next right onto Elsier."

When the gate went up, the driver made a noise in his throat. "Must be a ritzy neighborhood."

"I suppose so," she murmured, taking in the behemoth custom homes on either side of the street surrounded by elaborate, manicured landscaping. The neighborhood she and Wesley had grown up in had been nice, but it paled in comparison to this one, where Randolph had purchased a new home for him and Valerie and Prissy to live in. And Birch, the man Randolph had hired as a caretaker for Valerie and Prissy when they'd lived in Las Vegas under assumed names. Birch came across as a mild-mannered guy, but Carlotta had seen him morph into a special-ops ninja when Liz Fischer had held them hostage and set the house on fire. The man had skills, and his presence in Vegas made sense because Randolph had been guarding against the day his cover was blown and the masterminds behind the Ponzi/counterfeiting/money-laundering scheme at Mashburn & Tully came gunning for him.

Which begged the question why the babysitter-bodyguard still lived with them. Although in light of Randolph's warning the day before about Walt Tully, maybe it was a good idea to keep Birch around, especially since her mother and Prissy were so attached to him.

"It's the white house on the left," she said to the driver, pointing.

He whistled low under his breath as he pulled into the circular driveway. "Cool crib."

"Thanks," she said, then climbed out.

Stairs and a cleverly designed ramp led to the front door, a reminder that Randolph had bought the expansive house, which was customizable for wheelchair access, when he'd been under the impression that Valerie had early onset dementia and seemed headed for further decline. Happily, after her condition had been properly diagnosed and treated, she'd regained her health completely. But the gesture had further endeared Randolph to Carlotta.

Emotions warred in her chest as she climbed the steps to the entrance. Some part of her wished she could learn something objectionable about Randolph so she could distance her heart from his—and to justify learning the identity of her real father.

The door opened and Valerie appeared. Always an attractive woman with a dark chin-length bob, since recovering she'd regained the sparkle in her eyes. She smiled wide and held out her arms. "Hello, darling. I'm so glad you stopped by."

"I should've called," Carlotta murmured, then went in for a hug.

"Nonsense," Valerie said, squeezing hard. When she pulled back, her expression was earnest. "Our home is your home."

The sentiment was heartfelt, but Carlotta was aware of the wall that remained between them.

"Come in," her mother said quickly, to fill the silence. "I've been wanting to ask you some advice about decorating."

"I'm sure you don't need my advice. I couldn't have decorated my home office nearly as well as you did."

"Wesley had a hand, too," Valerie said demurely. "But do you like it?"

"I love it, although now I need a job."

"You'll figure it out. Don't be in a hurry."

"Dad said the same thing."

Valerie's brow wrinkled. "When did you talk to your father?"

"Yesterday at the jail. I was visiting Peter, and he was meeting Wes's attorney."

"Oh... right."

But she could tell her mother hadn't known. She wondered if her parents were having problems because of Valerie's gift of the locket and her revelation. On the other hand, Randolph was probably accustomed to handling things without discussing them with his wife.

Everyone, it seemed, would have to adjust to a new normal.

She followed her mother inside, through a foyer and formal living room, taking in the classic décor with modern touches. She'd seen the house unfurnished, but Valerie had transformed the space.

"Everything is absolutely beautiful," Carlotta murmured. And although she understood why her parents wanted to move from the house where she'd grown up, this new home made her feel even more like an outsider.

"It's not finished," Valerie said. "But I'm going to take my time. After all, your father and I will probably spend the rest of our lives here." She blushed prettily. "You can't imagine how happy that makes me."

Carlotta felt a rush of affection for her mother. Valerie had made mistakes, but she'd certainly had her share of suffering. "That makes me happy, too." She craned her neck. "Where's Prissy?"

"She and Randolph are in the pool. Go on out and I'll bring some iced tea."

Carlotta made her way to a great room that looked out onto a stone lanai, lush backyard, and pool. When she caught sight of her little sister and her father splashing each other, she stopped to soak it in. Prissy's yellow lab puppy was in the water, too, barking and adding to the commotion. Her sister was the image of herself at nine years old, and she had fond memories of Randolph as a playful, adoring father.

She indulged a pang that her time with Randolph had been

interrupted by her parents' abrupt departure. But it appeared he adored his younger daughter.

His true daughter.

Carlotta pushed aside the petty thought, then opened the sliding door and stepped outside.

"Carlotta!" Prissy swam to the ladder and climbed out. She grabbed a towel to wrap around her little body, then ran over to Carlotta and threw her arms around her waist.

"Don't get your sister wet," Randolph chided as he pushed himself out of the pool. Fit and tan, he was the picture of vitality, except for the ugly scar from being shivved when he was temporarily imprisoned.

"I don't mind," Carlotta said, laughing. Prissy had been a shocking bonus of finding her parents, and the precocious girl had helped to bind them all together in the difficult aftermath of their reunion.

"Birch is on vacation," Prissy announced, making a face.

"He deserves one, don't you think?" Carlotta asked, then accepted a quick kiss from Randolph.

"I'm glad you came," he said.

She nodded, but she knew he sensed her awkwardness. She hadn't yet reached a point where she could pretend things were the same, but the situation didn't have to be adversarial.

"I like your dress," Prissy said.

"Thank you."

"Is it Lilly Pulitzer?"

Carlotta grinned. "It is."

"You two were cut from the same cloth," Randolph said with a laugh.

Carlotta's gaze flew to his.

"So much like your mother," he added lightly.

She wondered if their conversations would ever not be so emotionally charged.

"Do you want to see my room?" Prissy asked with a grin. "My closet is *awesome*."

"Of course, I want to see everything."

The puppy had climbed out, too. He came loping up to Carlotta, then stopped and shook himself, showering her and her sundress with cold water and the smell of wet dog.

"Jack!" she yelled, lifting her arms in annoyance.

"Jack!" Prissy shouted with excitement, then pounded across the patio toward the sliding glass door.

Carlotta looked up to see Jack Terry emerging next to her mother who carried a tray of drinks.

Her chest tightened at his unexpected appearance. The last time she'd seen him they were saying goodbye at the Atlanta airport after returning from Dallas. He'd insisted he needed to tell her something, and she'd thought—hoped—he was finally going to admit to having feelings for her. Instead he'd divulged the secret of her parentage, unaware she'd found out only days before. The double-whammy of realizing he didn't have feelings to confess and that he'd known all along Randolph wasn't her father had left her feeling as if she'd fallen off a building only to be run over by a truck.

"Hi, Prissy," he said, all smiles for his little admirer.

"Where have you been?" she demanded.

Carlotta smothered a smile.

"Locking up bad guys," he said easily. Then he glanced up. "Hi, Carlotta."

"Jack," she said, inclining her head. "What brings you here?"

"I came to speak to Randolph."

Randolph was pulling on a shirt over his trunks. "What's this about, Detective?"

"Walter Tully."

"Prissy, let's go inside," Valerie said cheerfully.

"I don't want to!"

"Why don't you make sure your room is tidy?" Carlotta suggested. "I'll be right up for a full tour."

"Okay," the girl intoned. Then she shook her finger at Jack. "If you don't come to see me more often, I'm going to marry someone else."

"Yes, ma'am," he said, standing to mock attention.

"Come on, Jack," Prissy said, calling to her puppy. He followed her obediently.

Valerie hesitated at the door and glanced at Carlotta.

"I'm staying," she said, then looked to Jack for concurrence.

He gave a curt nod, then waited until Valerie had closed the door before he spoke. "Sorry to barge in like this, but I'm working with the GBI on Walt Tully's case. I'm wondering if you have any insight on where he might be."

Randolph shifted his stance, then crossed his arms. The irony of the situation wasn't lost on Carlotta. Mere months ago Randolph had been the hunted man... now he was being consulted by the very detective who had reopened the investigation into his disappearance. "I assume you haven't found any evidence that he's left the country?"

"Right," Jack said. "We've checked car rentals, bus and train tickets, and every airport within five hundred miles, plus toll checkpoints on all the interstates leading out of the city. Did you ever hear him mention a getaway in a rural area, maybe a hunting cabin?"

Randolph gave a little laugh. "Walt's idea of roughing it was staying at the Ritz Carlton instead of the Four Seasons. Have you checked there?"

"We have his picture circulated to all regional hotels." One side of Jack's mouth lifted. "Even the fleabag varieties. So you don't see him hiking out of the city, or camping to avoid detection?"

"No. If I had to guess, I'd say he hasn't gone far." Randolph pulled on his chin in thought. "Are you monitoring the Mashburn & Tully offices? They're empty, right?"

"Right. We've checked there, and a new company is taking over the space this week."

Carlotta remembered her encounter with Tracey a few days ago. "What about his daughter's and son's homes?"

"We have the residences of his immediate family under surveillance," Jack said, "but so far, nothing. And we have his picture circulated to all real estate agencies and leasing agents. But the truth is, we can't cover all the bases. We might just have to wait until he makes a mistake."

Randolph nodded. "He will... eventually."

Jack offered up a flat smile. "I assume you'll let me know if he contacts you?"

"If Walt reaches out to me, Detective, it won't be for my help."

"You think he'd try to even the score?"

Randolph shrugged. "Walter Tully is a narcissist and life as he knows it has ended. That could make a man pretty unpredictable."

Jack nodded, then stuck out his hand. "I appreciate your time."

Randolph shook it. "Sure thing, Detective."

Jack looked at Carlotta. "Walk me out?"

Surprised, she nodded, then led him back through the house and outside to the steps. She was keenly aware of his big body moving beside hers, but she was determined to keep the conversation out of personal territory. "Has there been any news about Wes's girlfriend Meg?"

"Unfortunately, no."

"What do you think might've happened?"

His expression hardened. "I don't want to speculate, but it doesn't look good. Every day that passes means she's less likely to be found."

Carlotta made a mournful noise. "I don't think Wes could take it if something happened to her."

"Then we'll keep pushing the local cops and hope for the best."

She nodded, then wet her lips. "How's Liz Fischer?"

He averted his gaze, then shook his head. "Not good. Still in the psych ward, still being evaluated for her ability to stand trial. How about Peter?"

"He has a bail review hearing next week. He's hopeful the judge won't hold Walt's flight against him."

"I heard Peter's dad has connections to Max Reeder who knows all the magistrate judges, so I wouldn't be surprised if he pulls some strings."

"Senator Max Reeder, who's running for President?"

"One and the same."

The man was embroiled in an infidelity scandal that threatened his chances to become the party's nominee. Strangely, Carlotta had had a chance encounter with the woman who claimed she and Senator had engaged in a long-term affair.

Jack pulled his hand over his mouth. "Listen... I have a favor to ask."

Carlotta blinked. "Okay."

"I, uh, need to upgrade my wardrobe."

She schooled her face to mask her surprise—and amusement. "And you want my help?"

His color heightened. "I wouldn't want to give the commission to someone else."

She smiled. "That's nice of you, Jack, but I left Neiman's."

His eyebrows shot up. "When?"

"A few days ago. The bridal salon was cut out of the budget, along with my position. Instead of going back to the sales floor, I decided to look for something else."

"Wow, that's a big change."

She nodded, then gave him a pointed look. "Change is good."

He didn't respond, but from the tightening of his jaw, she surmised he knew to what—and to whom—she was referring.

"But I can still help you out, Jack."

"Would you?"

"Sure. What day did you have in mind?"

"I can't tomorrow, but what about the day after?"

"Sure, that works."

He smiled. "Good. Should I pick you up?"

That was too personal, she decided. "I'll meet you at mall. One o'clock?"

"It's a date." Then he blanched. "I mean... I'll see you then."

Carlotta nodded, then watched Jack stride to his car, climb in, and peel away... with more gusto than necessary?

CHAPTER 8

CARLOTTA'S SPIRITS lifted at the mere sight of the Moody's Cigar Bar sign. And from the crowded parking lot, she wasn't the only person who felt drawn to the funky, cool gathering place this evening. After a day of wandering around her new home office, feeling at loose ends, she'd texted Coop to meet her there and he'd happily agreed.

She opened the ornate door and walked into the cool interior that was straight out the 1920's in its art deco design. Professionals of all ages and walks of life gathered for the retro charm of the glass-fronted wooden cabinets stocked with a world-class selection of cigars and loose tobacco, and drinks with old fashioned names like Gimlet and Sidecar. Up a set of wide wooden stairs was the lounge for the hardcore smokers and observers. Speakeasys were back in vogue with the millennials, so beards and smart suits abounded. A few women, she was delighted to see, wore wide-legged pantsuits made from menswear textiles, and spectator oxfords. From her own closet she'd chosen a drop-waisted slip dress of pebbled gray satin and bronze Sigerson Morrison sandals. The thrill of getting dressed and seeing how others used clothes to express themselves made her miss working at Neiman's. Clothing had been her life.

Now what?

She slipped into a vacant seat at the bar, then smiled at Nathan, the bartender.

"Hi, Carlotta."

"Hi, Nathan. Is June around?" June Moody, proprietor of the bar, had been a source of comfort and inspiration to Carlotta since the first time she'd crossed its threshold.

"She'll be in later. What can I get for you?"

Feeling adventurous—or was it indecisive?—she said, "Surprise me."

With the scent of fragrant smoke riding the air, the urge for a cigarette was keen. She massaged the nicotine patch on the back of her arm in an effort to push through the craving. A check of the time showed Coop wouldn't arrive for a few minutes, so to keep her hands occupied, she slipped a notebook from her bag and opened it to the page she'd been working on, per instructions from Dr. Denton.

You seem to have a set of beliefs about what you can and can't do. Write down some of those absolutes... then question them.

After making columns for each, she was hard-pressed to come up with entries for the "Can Do" column. Finally she wrote *I can sell clothes.*

She stared at the lone sentence. Was it the only skill she had to show for thirty years of being alive?

Wes would say she was good at being messy... Jack would say she was good at meddling... Coop would say she was good at keeping him in suspense.

She didn't like this exercise, she decided. Glancing around for a distraction, she noticed a familiar face on the TV screen behind the bar—the attractive redhead who'd been on the Dallas flight. Carlotta leaned in to hear the reporter's voice.

"Georgia Senator Max Reeder, whose reputation came under fire after a woman came forward with claims of an affair, has recovered ground in the latest poll because his alleged mistress, Colleen Mason, has seemingly withdrawn from the public eye. The Senator's publicist said the frontrunner for his party's nomination for president and married father of five is considering a defamation suit against Mason, but would settle for a retraction and apology."

Carlotta pursed her mouth. So the woman had backed down—from pressure the Senator had exerted, or had she been untruthful from the beginning? Then she made a rueful noise. If Senator

Reeder had influence to spare, she hoped a little of it would fall Peter's way.

"Here you go," Nathan said, setting a yellowish drink in front of her. "A Gin Rickey—premium gin, lime juice, and soda water, on the rocks."

"Thanks." She sipped. "Ooh, yum."

"Enjoy."

When he slipped away, she turned back to her list. Moving to the "Can't Do" column, she wrote *I have no education... I'm not smart like Wes... I have no business sense... I'm terrible with finances... I have no boundaries... I have no discipline... I don't always exhibit good judgment...*

She stopped and scanned the list, feeling decidedly depressed.

"Ooh, that's a long but pretty face," Coop said near her ear.

She looked up and smiled. "Hello, you."

"Hello, you." He kissed her on the mouth, then slid onto the stool next to her, looking relaxed and handsome in dress jeans and a collared shirt. He gestured for Nathan to bring him a club soda, then nodded to her notebook with a teasing smile. "Are you writing in your diary?"

"No," she said, closing the notebook. "It's supposed to be a self-discovery exercise. My, um, therapist recommended it."

She waited for him to look surprised. Instead he pursed his mouth and nodded. "It's good that you're talking to a professional."

"You think I need to talk to a professional?"

He smiled. "It doesn't matter what anyone else thinks—it only matters what you think. But I don't know many people who've been through as much as you have." Then he angled his head. "Did something trigger all these changes you've made recently—seeing a therapist, quitting your job?"

Finding out I'm not who I thought I was. The words hovered on her tongue, but for some reason, she resisted telling Coop about the circumstances of her birth. It was irrational, but she was embarrassed for him to know. Of all people, Coop would be the most understanding... but she wanted him to think well of her and her family.

Because she loved him?

"I think I know what it is," Coop said.

She lifted an eyebrow. "You do?'

"Patricia's death is still bothering you, isn't it?"

Her lips parted in surprise, then she nodded. "Yes. I still don't believe it was an accident."

"Thought so." He reached over to pick up her hand. "You were coworkers, you were traveling together, and you found the body, so of course you feel as if you should do something." He ran his thumb over her palm. "But there's nothing to be done. It was a terrible accident, that's all."

She nodded and hoped her smile was convincing.

"Has there been any word about Wes's girlfriend?"

"No. And Jack said it doesn't look good, that the longer she's missing, the less likely she'll be found."

Coop reached for the glass of club soda and lime Nathan set in front of him. "When did you talk to Jack?"

Was that a note of jealousy in his voice? "I was visiting my parents yesterday, and Jack stopped by to ask Randolph if he had any ideas where Walt Tully might be. I asked him about Meg before he left."

"Ah. And how is Jack?"

"Good, I suppose. He got a promotion, he's liaising with the GBI now."

"Wow, that sounds like a big jump."

"It must be—he asked me to help him upgrade his wardrobe."

"Did he now?"

"He didn't realize I'd left Neiman's," she said, eager to let him know Jack wasn't in the know about things in her life. *Except he knows about Randolph.* "But I told him I'd help him shop for few things."

"That's nice of you," Coop said lightly.

"It's the least I can do for him coming to Dallas to shadow the investigation when Patricia was killed."

"Died," he said lightly. "When Patricia *died.*"

"Right," she said, then offered him a conciliatory smile. "I guess I've been ruminating on Patricia's death because I'm bored."

"If you're bored, I can put you and Hannah on the nursing home runs for the morgue. Those are pretty standard calls and, sadly, regular. Sometimes every day, sometimes less often."

"I'd be glad to have something useful to do while I put

together a resume." She grinned. "Can I put you down as a job reference?"

He grinned back. "Only if I can sexually harass you."

She laughed, enjoying the flirty banter. She studied his warm eyes and hot body. This man made her happy. He was solid, dependable...

"Hey, how did your friend's science experiment go?"

"Hm?"

"The, um, *sample* that needed to be rehydrated?"

... and trusting.

"Oh, that." Carlotta pulled her hand free to pick up her drink and take a deep, tangy sip. "Hopefully that situation will all be resolved soon."

CHAPTER 9

CARLOTTA GLANCED at her phone to check the time, then texted Jack.

Change your mind?

In a few seconds, her phone vibrated.

That could apply to a lot of things

She frowned, but before she could dissect his words, another text came in.

But no, I didn't change my mind about the clothes, just running late. Parking.

She shook her head—Jack was good at cryptic references and innuendoes. But she wasn't going to let their relationship drift into No Man's Land again.

Since she had her phone out, she leaned into the high top table at their designated meeting spot inside the mall and swiped over to review the photos she'd taken of Patricia's hotel suite. Her conversation with Coop last night had only driven the incident deeper into her subconscious. She couldn't stop thinking about how she'd slumbered in the hotel room across the hall on a pillow-top mattress all night while Patricia had lain on the cold, hard bathroom floor.

After the body had been removed, she'd sneaked back into the room and used her phone to take individual shots, stitching them together for panoramic photos. Patricia's bed was turned down but looked to be unslept in, and her belongings were strewn throughout the bedroom and the bathroom, although it was difficult to know which items might've been disturbed by the first responders. Patricia's two suitcases were open on valet stands, both of them half unpacked. On the table in the sitting room were the remains of what looked like two meals, although she now wished she'd gotten closer shots. Maybe Hannah was right and Patricia had simply ordered enough comfort food to soothe her wounded pride after her dream date had fizzled.

The next pictures were in the bathroom where Carlotta had found her lying face up, her head in a pool of dried blood. It had been surreal to see her like that, so still, her eyes wide and unseeing. Carlotta inadvertently shuddered, wondering what Patricia had seen just before she died—had she, as the police theorized, simply fallen hard and lay there dazed staring at the ceiling while her brain shut down from the blow... or had she seen the face of the person who'd killed her?

On the vanity was a jumble of beauty products, many of them toppled, presumably as she'd fallen. Plus the hotels miniature toiletries, and Patricia's black makeup case. Carlotta had carefully opened the case and taken photos of the contents. Something about the artfully arranged products struck her as sad, that Patricia had so carefully packed for the Dallas trip with the hope of making a good impression for her career and on the man she'd arranged to meet, and instead had lost her life in such a random way.

Carlotta flashed back to when they'd gone through security at the Atlanta airport and Patricia, high on anxiety meds, had accused the TSA agent of stealing her phone. He hadn't, of course, but the tense situation had set the tone for the trip. When the phone was found in Patricia's bag, they'd had to make a run for it and were the last passengers to board the plane. She and Patricia had bickered throughout the flight. Looking back, she wished she'd been more tolerant instead of alienating the woman further. In many ways, she and Patricia had much in common—a privileged upbringing that had been yanked out from under them, and Randolph had been at the center of it. Patricia's parents had lost everything years ago in the scandal Mashburn & Tully had then blamed on her father. She only hoped they were at least in line for restitution once the partners had been prosecuted.

Assuming Walt Tully was ever found.

She swiped back and forth to review the pictures, stopping again on the picture of the vanity contents. Something about it seemed off... but she couldn't put her finger on it...

"Hi, there."

At the sound of Jack's voice, she jumped guiltily and dropped her phone. They reached for it at the same time, but he got to it first. She yanked it out of his hand and he gave a little laugh.

"If you're trying to hide nude selfies, Carlotta, remember, I've seen it all."

She frowned and stowed her phone, grateful he hadn't seen the crime scene photos. "Don't start, Jack."

He lifted his hands. "Sorry. You make it so easy." Then he sighed. "Why'd you have to wear a red dress?"

She glanced down at her strappy sundress. "What's wrong with red?"

"It looks too good on you."

She gave a little scoff, but couldn't control the flush that warmed her cheeks. "There's no need for flattery, Jack, I'm happy to help you shop."

He winced. "I'm glad one of us is happy about it. Sorry I was late, I was on an international call regarding Wes's girlfriend."

She bit into her lip. "Any word?"

He shook his head. "The locals are taking it more seriously, but there's so much ground to cover and most of the people who were with her around the time she disappeared have left the area. It's like looking for a needle in a haystack, except we don't even have a haystack."

She made a mournful sound. "Wes is walking around like a zombie, and I know her parents are losing their minds, especially with all the stories in the news about young women disappearing who are never heard from again."

"Let's just hope this story has a better ending." But his expression was grim.

She nodded. "So... tell me about this new job of yours."

"Lots of desk work," he grumbled, "but when I go out in the field, I need to look... better."

She surveyed his off-work uniform of form-fitting jeans, black T-shirt, and black cowboy boots. As tall and thick as a tree with dark hair and golden-hued eyes, the man was lethal. Every woman who walked by cast her glance his way, no matter the age. The thought flitted through her mind that the only way he could look better was to be wearing fewer clothes, but she didn't say it. He didn't need a reason to be more cocky.

"Do I have a budget to work with?" she asked.

"I got a pay bump, but don't bankrupt me."

"Enough of a pay bump to improve your housing situation?"

He frowned. "Why would I want to do that?"

Darn it—foiled. She knew next to nothing about Jack, didn't even know where he lived. Yet another reason why she was better off with Coop. "Come on… let's get started."

"I'm all yours."

Carlotta bit her tongue, then pulled out her notebook. "We're going to need pants, shirts, jackets, ties, belts, shoes, socks, a suit, underwear, and overcoat. Also, do you have a briefcase?"

He scowled. "I don't need a damn purse."

She lifted an eyebrow. "I thought you wanted my help."

He wiped his hand over his mouth, then sighed. "Okay, okay."

She smiled. "Atta boy. Now… follow me." Carlotta shouldered her bag, then led him to the first store, a men's clothier. "We'll get pants here."

"I assumed you'd want me to buy everything from Neiman's."

"Some things, absolutely. But this clothier is better for big and tall men, and they use premium fabric for their pants. They'll look good and last a long time."

"As long as I don't have to do this again anytime soon."

"I promise this will be less painful than getting shot at." She greeted the male sales associate, then gestured to Jack. "He needs slacks, flat front, straight leg, no cuff, with ease in the thigh, and button rear pockets."

"Do you have a fabric in mind?" he asked Carlotta.

"Cotton, with some stretch, maybe two or three percent elastane."

He led them to a section of slacks, then pointed. "That would be these two racks. What color?"

"Solid black and grey, and the brown glen plaid," she said, pointing, "Also, the indigo blue and the sand."

"Waist?"

"Thirty-four."

"Inseam?"

"Thirty-six."

"Rise?"

"Is your long rise one-half inch longer than the regular rise?"

"Yes, ma'am."

She sized up Jack's crotch area. "Long rise, please."

Jack coughed lightly, then smiled. She shot him daggers.

The man removed the garments from the racks. "What else, ma'am?"

"That's all for now. He'll try those."

"Right this way."

She gestured for Jack to follow the man, then walked behind him to the louvered door of the dressing room that was open on the top and the bottom.

The associate hung the pants inside, then stepped out.

Jack glanced at Carlotta. "You coming in?"

Her chest expanded with a proprietary feeling, but she'd been there before. Jack had a way of making her feel as if she was his girlfriend when it wasn't the case. "No," she said cheerfully. "Just come out when you're ready. Try the blue ones first, please."

"Okay," he said in a voice that sounded dubious, then closed the door.

She heard the unzipping and unbuttoning of his pants and squeezed her eyes shut not to remember the times he'd shed his pants to crawl in bed with her. She was going to have to get a grip or she'd never get through the day with her sanity intact.

"Hey," he said with surprise. "Not bad." He opened the door, then lifted his T-shirt to push one finger between the waistband and his flat stomach.

She swallowed hard—not bad indeed. "Do they feel good?"

"Yeah, nice and comfy."

The man moved like an athlete, even during sex. Her face warmed and her hairline grew moist. "Sit in the chair," she said, pointing, "to see if they bind or pinch anywhere."

He did. "No, they're perfect."

They'd made love in a chair once or twice. "Put your hands in the pockets."

He did. "Nice and deep."

She decided she needed to be somewhere else while he was taking off and putting on pants. "Okay, try on the rest to make sure they fit the same, and I'll meet you at the counter."

She walked away fanning her neck and trying to push illicit memories from her mind. It was to be expected considering their history, but she could do this—she could.

While he finished trying on pants, she chose three leather belts... and when her mind moved toward him binding her wrists with them, she began to hum, ignoring the strange looks from the associate helping her.

A few minutes later, Jack emerged and met her at the counter with the slacks. "They all fit great."

"Because this is a quality store," she said. "But don't ever assume—try on everything before you take it home, even if it's a duplicate of something else that fits."

"Got it."

"He'll take these," she said, smiling at the sales associate. "Do you have any specials today?"

"With such a sizable purchase, I think we can throw in one of the belts," he said.

"Thank you, that's very generous," she said, beaming.

"It's a pleasure to wait on such an educated customer," the man returned.

Jack winked at her, then handed over his credit card. When they left, Jack looked a little dazed. "That's the fastest I've ever been in and out of a clothing store."

"That's because I know what I'm doing," she said lightly. "But we still have a long way to go."

Staying true to her list, they went to Nordstrom's next for shirts and ties where watching Jack flex in and out of garments had her gritting her teeth. To remind herself her romantic intentions lay elsewhere, she found a funky tie she thought would look good with Coop's brown eyes and paid for it separately at the register.

Jack eyed the purchase. "Coop will like it," he said breezily.

"I hope so," she said with just as much air.

Next they moved on to Neiman's for jackets and a suit tailored for the wide shoulders and back that she'd clawed more than once in her passion. Then to Allen Edmonds for respectable dress shoes and a pair of low-heeled modern-looking boots for his immense feet that had her remembering his proportions all too graphically. On to Macy's for socks and underwear (she knew what he liked) and a smart all-weather overcoat. And finally to a luggage store to buy a heavy duty Briggs & Riley briefcase that Jack actually liked. Throughout she kept things moving at a rapid clip to quell the urge to look at—and touch—him. If the conversation veered into the personal realm, she steered it back to retail. At every store she had coupons, had hit a sale, or managed to get bonus merchandise thrown in.

"Wow," Jack said when they stowed the last of the bags in his off-duty SUV. "That was less painful than I expected."

Carlotta angled her head. "Are you saying you had fun shopping?"

"I wouldn't go that far, but you did make it more pleasant than I thought it would be, and I still have a little room left on my credit card. Want to grab a bite to eat?"

Her lips parted—a shared meal seemed too... intimate. "Um..."

"It's the least I can do to repay you," he said quickly.

"Thanks, but I promised Wes I'd be home for dinner. I think he needs the company right now."

Something flashed in Jack's eyes—disappointment, or relief? "Of course. Give you a ride home?"

His body pulled on hers. She inhaled, exhaled. "No, thanks. I need to run some errands, then I'll catch the train."

"Okay. Thanks for today." He scratched his temple. "You're really good at this. You should be a professional shopper, or whatever they're called."

"A personal shopper," she said with a smile. "That's nice, but I don't know anything about running a business."

He gave a sharp laugh. "When has not knowing something ever stopped you?"

She opened her mouth, but nothing came out.

Jack shrugged. "It was just a thought. See you around?"

She found her voice. "Sure."

He hesitated for two heartbeats, then climbed into his vehicle and drove away.

Carlotta stared after him, then pulled out her notebook where she'd written down all the things that were strikes against her.

Then she applied Dr. Denton's advice to question her limiting beliefs.

I have no education. But I have experience.

I'm not smart like Wes. But I'm resourceful.

I have no business sense. But I know what customers want.

I'm terrible with finances. But I'm good with people.

I have no boundaries. But I'm a risk taker.

I have no discipline. But I'm getting better.

I don't always exercise good judgement.

She stopped on the last one and worked her mouth back and forth. Six out of seven wasn't bad.

Carlotta closed the notebook, then went back into the mall, through Neiman's, and threaded her way to Lindy's office. To her surprise and delight, Quentin Gallagher was sitting outside her former boss's office, pouring over pricing spreadsheets. He looked up and his face broke into a huge smile. "Carlotta. So nice to see you."

"You, too, Quentin... Lindy told me good things about you."

"I'm really enjoying working here. Thanks again for the endorsement."

"Happy to do it. Is Lindy available?"

Lindy suddenly appeared at her office door. "I thought that was your voice, Carlotta. Are you back?"

"Not necessarily," Carlotta said. "But I have a proposition."

Lindy looked intrigued. "I'm all ears."

CHAPTER 10

"A FREELANCE personal shopper?" Hannah asked as Carlotta led her down the hallway of the townhouse. "That's the perfect job for you!"

"I know, right? It was actually Jack's idea."

"Ugh, don't give that man credit for something you would've figured out on your own in a day or two."

"That's the problem, I still don't have it figured out. It's one thing to say I'm a personal shopper—it's another to stir up enough business to make a living at it."

"You're smart, though, to arrange commissions from the stores where you shop so it won't cost the customer anything extra."

"It's a good deal for the store—they would pay a commission on the sale anyway, and this way they don't have to pay my overhead as an employee."

"It could be the future of brick and mortar retail," Hannah said. "Plus you won't have to deal with twats like Tracey Tully Lowenstein."

"I had a run-in with her when I went to clean out my locker."

"Please tell me you punched her in the titty."

"Sorry, I didn't." Carlotta stopped with her hand on the door of her new home office. "Wait til you see my new digs."

"I hope there's a TV because I'm missing my favorite cooking show."

She opened the door. "Ta-da!"

"Wow," Hannah said, walking into her parents' transformed bedroom. The mixture of white walls and dark hardwood floors gave it a cool, Key West vibe. A black desk with guest chairs and matching bookcases set off one side of the room, while a red loveseat and chairs around a coffee table suggested a meeting space. In the corner a TV had been mounted near the ceiling. "The little shit did all this for you?"

"With some design help from my mom, but yeah, it was Wes's idea."

"It's the least he owes you for all the sleep you've lost over him."

Carlotta made a rueful noise. "Still losing, you mean."

"No word about his girlfriend yet?"

"No."

"Damn, do you think she's been murdered?"

"Don't even say that."

"Sorry, but it's not looking good."

"I know," Carlotta murmured. "But Wes hasn't given up hope yet."

Hannah picked up the remote control and found the Food Network. Then she stood in place and turned a full circle. "With an office this nice, you have no choice but to start your own business."

Carlotta bit into her lip. "I like the sound of it, but I admit I'm overwhelmed. I don't know where to start."

"Take a digital marketing class. I did, and I think I'm on to something good."

Recalling Hannah's bedroom tripod and backdrop, she asked, "When are you going to tell me about this business of yours?"

"When I get good at it," Hannah said vaguely, studying the screen where a woman was removing a shiny brown bird from the oven. "Man, doesn't that look good?"

Carlotta angled her head. "Sure. Is it a turkey?"

Hannah flailed her arms. "It's a *duck*. How can you not see that?"

"Because it's not quacking?"

"You're hopeless. Anyway, now's a great time to start an online business. You can do everything remotely—blog, make videos, get a social media following and a mailing list, attract advertisers, launch a podcast, sell products and services."

"You might as well be speaking a foreign language."

Hannah scoffed. "It's not hard, it just takes time." She looked around. "And some equipment. Where's your computer?"

"My laptop belonged to Neiman's, and the terms of Wes's probation prohibits him being around computers."

"Oh, yeah—I forgot the dumbass broke into the courthouse database."

"But his community service is over for those charges, so hopefully that'll change soon."

"Meanwhile, use your phone to learn from people who are already doing what you want to do. Follow them in social media. Sign up for their mailing list. Go on YouTube. Start listening to podcasts. And read a book or two."

Carlotta was jotting hurried notes. "Thanks for the advice... I'll get started right away." Then she cleared her throat. "Hey, were you able to get the security tape from the hotel?"

Hannah turned a frown her way. "Still working on it."

"Great. Hannah... does Chance know about your, um, business?"

"No. Why would he?"

"I don't know, maybe because the two of you are married? By the way, when are you going to break the news to your family?"

"It's all part of the plan," Hannah said. "If this business takes off, I won't need to work for my father, and then I can figure out a way to reveal Chance without fear of being cut off."

Carlotta smirked. "I thought Chance had a trust fund."

"He does, but his annuity isn't enough to live on without all his little sordid side businesses. And your dad pays him shit at that driving range." Then she stopped. "Sorry—should I still say 'your dad'?"

Carlotta nodded, then sighed. "In fact, I'm having second thoughts about trying to find the identity of my biological father."

Hannah shrugged. "So, when you get the results back, you'll have your genetic makeup... but nothing says you have to plug it into the global family tree to see if you have relatives."

"You're right. I'll wait and make up my mind then."

Hannah glanced at her watch. "Is it time to go to the nursing home yet to pick up Mrs. Stern? I need to be back home by six to... work on my business."

A scheduled peep show? "Coop said we should wait until after lunch so the other residents can give her a sendoff, but we can leave now." She reached for her purse.

"I hate the nursing home pickups," Hannah groused as they walked back through the townhouse. "Give me a crime scene any day."

"Hannah."

"Do I at least get to ogle Coop? Are we taking her to the morgue?"

"No. To a funeral home, I think."

"Ugh."

"Hannah, be nice." Carlotta looked through the side window to make sure Mrs. Winningham wasn't in her yard. "Okay, we can make a run for it."

They hurried through the door, then sprinted to Hannah's van.

They almost made it. "Yoo-hoo, Carlotta!"

"Can't talk now, Mrs. Winningham!"

"We're going to get a dead body!" Hannah shouted.

When they were settled in the van, Carlotta looked over. "Thanks. That's something else she can grill me about the next time I'm outside. Seriously, though, thanks for doing this. I can use the extra cash until I figure out how I'm going to support myself. And it helps Coop."

Hannah started the van. "No problem. What's going on with you and Coop, anyway?"

"We're... taking it slow."

"Why? He's the perfect man! I can't believe you wasted so much time with Peter Ashford and Jack Terry when Coop was standing right there with his tongue hanging out."

"Nice visual." She hesitated, then said, "Actually... I've been thinking about telling Coop that I love him."

Hannah whooped. "It's about fucking time!" Then she stopped. "Wait—why haven't you?"

Carlotta pressed her lips together.

"You don't know if you love him?" Hannah pressed. "You don't know if you love him," she repeated, this time a statement. "Listen, Carlotta, you know I'm rooting for you two, but if you tell

Coop you love him, you gotta mean it because he will absorb it to the bone."

Carlotta sighed. "I know."

Hannah sighed. "Let's go get Dead Granny."

CHAPTER 11

"WREN, YOU'RE up!" The woman at the counter shouted.

Wes dragged his butt out of the waiting room chair, then put one foot in front of the other to move himself forward.

"Hey," she said as he walked by, "I thought the last time you were here was the last time you were here."

"I'm back," he said half-heartedly, too depressed even to flirt with the sour woman like he usually did.

He made his way to his probation officer E. Jones's office, not wanting to be there, yet glad to have something to do today other than sit and ruminate on how many ways Meg might've been tortured before someone had thrown her slender body into a ravine where it would never be found.

He simply couldn't contemplate a world without her in it.

Wes stopped and rapped on the door, frowning at his bandaged fingertips. The bitter hand sanitizer hadn't helped to prevent him from biting his nails, in fact, he'd developed a taste for the awful stuff. He was hoping the bandages would be a barrier long enough for them to heal, or until Meg was found. At this point he was in danger of chewing off his fingerprints.

And buying enough oxy to take him to the moon.

"Come in."

He opened the door, then slid inside. Eldora Jones was watering a plant on a cabinet next to the lone window in her office. She wore a peach-colored blouse and a brown skirt that on anyone else would've looked matronly, but she managed to make it look hot. A little smile played on her face when she looked up. She seemed happier, and he hoped she was over her lunkhead of a fiancé Leonard, a drug running thug who'd gotten himself killed.

"Hi, Wes, have a seat."

He sat, then waited for her to finish. He put a finger in his mouth, but lowered it when he encountered latex.

She abandoned the watering can, then came back to sit at her desk. "How are you—" She stopped, and her brow furrowed. "What's wrong?"

A lump formed in his throat and he blinked back sissy tears. "Pretty much everything."

"Take a deep breath, and tell me."

He dragged air into his quivering lungs, then told her about Meg vanishing while biking through Ireland. "It's been over two weeks," he said in a broken voice. "I'm scared she's... never coming back."

Her face was drawn. "I've been hearing about the Vincent girl on the local news, but I didn't make the connection. I believe I ran into the two of you at an event."

He nodded. She'd been there with Leonard.

E. smiled. "So you like this girl?"

"I love her," he blurted. "She loves me, too. I should be over there looking for her. I need to get this damn ankle bracelet removed."

"I'd help you if I could, but only your attorney can make this happen."

He wiped his eyes and nose on his sleeve. "He's supposed to be working on it."

"Then I'm afraid you'll have to be patient."

"Can you at least make a phone call?"

She nodded. "Yes... I can to that."

He sat forward in the chair. "How much trouble will I be in if I violate probation?"

"A lot." She shook her head. "Don't do it, Wes, not now when you're so close to having your record cleared. The assistant D.A. and I pulled in a lot of favors to get you the community service deal to work at the morgue. Don't mess that up."

She glanced down to his ravaged hands. "How are you holding

up?"

"Not well," he said, then raised blurry eyes to hers. His knee was jumping.

"Do you feel as if you might fall back into a bad habit?"

He put a finger in his mouth and gnawed on a bandage. "Maybe."

"Do you have someone you can talk to? Your father, mother... sister?"

Carlotta was dealing with her own emotional trauma after finding out Randolph wasn't her real dad... and his mother had only just recovered from a serious health issue. And not only did his father not give a damn about Meg being lost, but he seemed irritated that Wes was distracted from playing cards. "Not about this."

"You seemed to be close to Dr. Craft at the morgue."

He nodded. "Yeah, Coop is a recovered alcoholic. He would understand."

"Have you talked to him about your community service hours?"

"Not yet. I found out about Meg after you and I last met... and I haven't been able to think about anything else." Other than oxy.

"I understand," she said. "But promise me you'll talk to Coop soon?"

He nodded, then stood to leave.

"And Wes... keep me posted on Meg. I'll be thinking about you both."

Wes tried to smile, then trudged back through the stagnate office and outside into the searing heat. He calculated how fast he could pedal to the corner in Little Five Points where the guy in the brown knit hat cruised around on an electric scooter serving up oxy.

"Hiya, Wes."

He turned his head to see a familiar black Town Car sitting near the curb and the ugly mug of its hefty driver sticking out the window. "Mouse!"

"Hey, Little Man. I was cruising by and recognized your bike chained up. How are you?"

Wes bit down on his tongue to stem another flood of embarrassing tears. "Dude, I've been better."

Mouse's big face creased in concern. "Sorry to hear that. I was about to go get a burger. Wanna join me?"

Wes was so relieved, he wanted to fall to his knees. "Yeah... sounds good."

CHAPTER 12

AT THE sound of the doorbell, Carlotta lifted her head from the book she'd been reading and glanced at her watch. She decided Hannah must've arrived early for their nursing home run. Pushing to her feet, she stretched her arms overhead to stretch her shoulders. All morning she'd been bent over books she'd bought on starting an at-home business. She was learning all kinds of new terms like "personal brand building," "affiliate marketing," "point of service payment processing," and "multi-prong strategies." Her brain was reaching overload, but she felt... *exhilarated.*

Exhilarated to be focused on something other than the drama of her family and the drama of her love life.

She walked down the hallway, stopping to close the door to Wes's bedroom that sat ajar. Their rule was as long as he kept a snake in his room, the door stayed closed. But she'd let it slip this time because she knew his mind was elsewhere. She dearly hoped Meg came home safely, for her family's sake and for Wes's. She wasn't sure his tender heart could withstand that kind of blow, and she worried about him turning back to drugs.

At the front door, she expected to see Hannah standing on the stoop. Instead a package delivery person stood there. She opened the door and offered a smile to the woman, then signed for a padded envelope. When she saw the return address was The Saxler House hotel in Dallas, her pulse spiked—Patricia's found phone.

She backtracked to her office to open the envelope. Inside the phone was contained in a zip-top bag and from the bits of unidentified goop on the phone, it hadn't been cleaned after it was found underneath the hotel dumpster. Patricia's initials were on the case and the screen was cracked. She decided to leave it inside the plastic bag to try to preserve as many fingerprints as possible just in case a killer had removed it from her room and tossed it. The other explanation was that Patricia had simply lost the phone and whoever found it had used it until the battery died, then tossed it. Patricia had admitted she misplaced it often.

The phone was a different brand than her own, and needed a special charger. Since it was the same brand as Hannah's she could borrow her charger when she arrived, although she hated having to wait to see if the phone held anything useful. Then she remembered the bag of items she'd removed from Patricia's work locker. She'd hung onto the contents thinking she'd return them to Patricia's parents when she returned the phone—perhaps Patricia had kept a spare charger at work.

She retrieved the bag and was relieved to find a charger. She opened the plastic bag that held the phone and carefully inserted the cable, gratified when a charging symbol appeared on the screen. While the phone charged, she sorted through the photos from Patricia's locker, just in case the woman had kept a naughty picture or two she wouldn't want her parents to see.

There weren't any X-rated pictures, but one photo did stop Carlotta. It was a picture of her and Patricia taken at the Wedding World Expo when they'd worked the Neiman's booth. She was smiling, but Patricia was practically beaming, her head bent toward Carlotta's. Carlotta's heart squeezed at the knowledge that the picture had meant enough to Patricia that she'd kept it.

When the phone had charged to twenty-five percent, she powered it on, pressing the buttons through the plastic. Thankfully much of the screen could be read despite the crack, but when a keypad came up and she was asked to enter a passcode, she groaned. She tried the usual suspects of 1, 2, 3, 4, and 0, 0, 0, 0. She knew after a certain amount of attempts she'd be locked out.

Then she recalled the rooms at the hotel required a four-digit passcode to open the door using an app, and Patricia's passcode had been 3, 3, 7, 6. Hoping it was a passcode she used often,

Carlotta punched in the number…

And the home screen appeared. Carlotta nearly cheered.

She brought up the call app and clicked on the tab for recent activity, then carefully wrote down each phone number for unknown calls. Carlotta reasoned they could be spam calls, or calls from people or companies who didn't realize she'd died. Carlotta saw her own name and phone number for the morning she'd found the body—she remembered frantically calling when she'd realized she'd overslept. Hers was no doubt one of the handful of voice messages that hadn't yet been played. She pressed the button to dial Patricia's voicemail service and sure enough, her panicked message was the first one. Hearing her own voice brought back the events of that awful day with jarring clarity. Thank goodness Jack had hopped on a plane and held her hand through the initial investigation.

Although now she realized he'd done it out of guilt for keeping the secret of her parentage from her, and with the intention of telling her.

The next message was from Lindy Russell, asking Patricia to please call, that Carlotta was looking for her and the morning meeting was on pause. The rest of the messages were either spam or courtesy calls from companies about an overdue payment.

Next she went to the texting app. There were a handful of unread texts, all of them from John Smythe.

I'm sorry for lying to you, I just wanted to meet you
Will you please talk to me? I miss you.
Can we at least be friends?
Are u ok?
I guess you don't want to talk

So either John Smythe from the dating app didn't know Patricia was dead, or he'd sent the texts to lead investigators astray. Patricia hadn't saved their previous text conversations so it was still unclear what John Smythe had lied about.

She wrote down the Dallas area number he'd texted from and checked it against the list of numbers Patricia had received calls from or placed herself, but it appeared they'd only texted.

The only other text conversation saved was the one between herself and Patricia from the evening prior to Carlotta finding her body.

U were right about John. Happy?

What happened?

I'll tell u tomorrow.

I'm at the restaurant bar if u want to come by. The bartender is cute.

No, thanks. Going to unpack.

I can come up if u want to talk.

But Patricia hadn't responded, not to the last text and not to her knock on the door when she'd gone up to try to convince her to come to the bar. Gooseflesh raised on her arms. Had Patricia been dead then? Had someone been in her room listening to Carlotta on the other side of the door?

Next she scrolled through the apps and found only one dating app—likely the one on which Patricia had met John. But when Carlotta opened the app, a message displayed that the account had been deactivated for lack of payment.

Last she pulled up Patricia's photos, again to go through them and delete any that might hurt or offend her parents. There were mostly selfies, and only a couple suggestive enough that Carlotta hit the delete button. The rest of the photos looked to have been taken at family get togethers—she was obviously close to her parents. But it seemed a little sad that Patricia didn't have pictures with friends or texts from friends. Even her contacts list was short compared to the number of contacts Carlotta had in her phone.

Her doorbell sounded again. She set aside Patricia's phone and this time when she walked to the door, Hannah was standing on the stoop. She opened the door, held up her phone, and took a picture.

"What the hell?" Hannah asked, drawing back.

"I don't have very many pictures of you."

"Okay, weird. Are you ready to go to the geezer kennel?"

"Hannah, have a little respect. We're going to be old someday."

"Speak for yourself."

"Would you mind if we made a stop first at Patricia's parents' house? I want to drop off the things from her work locker, and her phone arrived this morning."

"No problem. Did you find anything good on the phone?"

"A number for the online date she met, and I'm going to call the other numbers on the way to see if one of them belongs to Trevor Biondi."

"He's the guy from the taxi stand?"

"Right."

"By the way, by "good" I mean did you find any good porn on there?"

"No."

"Hey, I'm only asking because if we do find out one of these guys did her in, maybe we can identify him from a dick pic."

"Or maybe we can identify him from hotel security footage. How's that going?"

Hannah frowned. "Working on it. Do you know how antsy people get when the boss's daughter calls for a favor, then tells them to keep it a big, fat secret? They think it's a sting."

"Then why don't you tell your father?"

"Because then he'll tell the police, and Jack will put you in time out." Then she raised an eyebrow. "Or maybe that's what you want?"

Carlotta gave her a withering look, then gathered her purse and the bag of Patricia's things, placing the woman's phone inside. After locking the door, they made their way to Hannah's van.

"Where's your nosy neighbor today?" Hannah asked.

"Inside her house, writing down the make, model, and license plate number of your van."

"Why?"

"Apparently she keeps a log of cars that come and go from here, so she has proof when she calls the police to complain about us."

"Crazy follows you around," Hannah said.

Carlotta gave her friend a pointed look.

"I'm the good kind of crazy."

She laughed as Hannah turned the van around in the driveway.

"Where do Patricia's parents live?"

"Not far. Head toward Piedmont." Working from the list of calls from unknown numbers on Patricia's phone, she used her own phone to call each one. As she suspected, most were robocalls.

"No luck?" Hannah asked.

"No, but I have a hunch about this next number. It's a Dallas area code and from the timestamp, it came in after Patricia texted me that her date had failed and she was going to unpack. On her phone it has a green incoming arrow next to it, so that means she took the call, right?"

"Right. How long did it last?"

Carlotta consulted Patricia's phone. "Less than two minutes. Is that enough time to arrange a hookup?"

Hannah gave her deadpan look. "Yes. And it's sad you don't know that."

Carlotta ignored her.

"If he answers, what are you going to say?"

"I don't know, I guess I'll wing it."

"Put it on speaker."

After punching in the number, Carlotta held her breath. After one ring, an automated message clicked on. "Your call cannot be completed as dialed. Please check the number and redial."

Carlotta did, but got the same message. "Dammit, I just know this is—was—the man's number."

"A police officer could check," Hannah said in a dry voice.

"If the police had done their job I wouldn't have to be doing this." She looked up. "Take the next left to get to the Alexanders'."

Hannah flipped on her signal and when she made the turn, she said, "This isn't a great neighborhood."

"Patricia's parents lost their life savings with Mashburn & Tully, like your folks did." Except Hannah's parents had bounced back in a big way.

"That sucks. Think they'll get anything back once the partners are prosecuted?"

"Maybe... hopefully."

"Assuming Tracey's papa is found and extradited."

"Tracey isn't the nicest person," Carlotta murmured, "but she can't help who her father is. I was in her shoes once." She lifted her hand and pointed. "That's the address, the blue house."

"You've been here?"

"No, but I sent a sympathy card."

Hannah pulled in behind an unpretentious sedan. "Looks like someone is home."

"I won't be long."

She shouldered the bag holding Patricia's things, then opened the door and jumped down. Her pulse picked up as she approached the front door that was, sadly, adorned with a withered wreath, probably a gift from a thoughtful neighbor. She rang the doorbell and waited, glancing around at the small house that was a little shabby around the edges. The Alexanders lived modestly.

The door opened and Laura Alexander squinted. "Yes?"

"Hi, Mrs. Alexander. I'm Carlotta Wren. I worked with Patricia at Neiman's."

A small smile lifted the woman's mouth. "Oh, yes, Patricia was happy to be working for you. And you were with her when she—" She broke off abruptly.

"Yes," Carlotta said quickly. "Patricia was a good person and a good employee. I'll miss her."

Laura composed herself. "I know your parents, of course. And for the record, I never blamed your father for what happened. I'm glad his name was cleared."

"That's very kind of you to say." Carlotta held out the bag. "I emptied Patricia's locker at work and thought you might want her things."

The woman's brow furrowed. "Actually, I don't." Her eyes filled with tears. "It was nice of you to bring them by, but I can't take any more reminders that my daughter is no longer here. I'm overwhelmed with clearing out her apartment."

"I understand," Carlotta said gently, then patted the bag. "I'll go through these things if you like and donate what others might find useful. And I'm happy to help you with Patricia's other possessions if you need a hand."

Ms. Alexander looked relieved, then opened the door wider and nodded to two large unopened boxes sitting in the foyer. "These arrived today from the hotel where she was staying." Her voice was choked. "I can't bear to open them."

Something akin to excitement barbed through Carlotta's chest. "Would you like for me to take them? I can go through them and pull out anything valuable, like jewelry, that you might want to keep."

The woman's expression lifted. "Would you? And find a home for her clothes?"

"Absolutely." She waved to Hannah for assistance, then the

two of them carried the boxes to the van. Mrs. Alexander thanked them so profusely, Carlotta fought off guilty pangs. She was, after all, trying to find justice for Patricia.

As Hannah backed down the driveway, she gave a little laugh. "Unbelievable."

"What?"

"You have pictures from the crime scene, DNA from the crime scene, and now, everything from the crime scene itself, including Patricia's phone. Jesus, Carlotta, you're basically your own CSI episode."

Carlotta smiled to herself. *Plus ten points.*

CHAPTER 13

ANY OTHER day Wesley would've been happy to be standing in the lobby of the county morgue, waiting for Coop and the chance to work side by side with the man who'd been instrumental in spotting and correcting his mother's dementia misdiagnosis.

But today his mind was miles away—four thousand miles, to be exact. He'd called Mark at least fifty times but the asshole hadn't picked up. He'd resorted to surfing online for any mention of Meg's disappearance, but the news items were vague and some had a skeptical tone. Worse, the mentions had dwindled to nearly nothing. People were losing interest—and hope.

To pass the time while he waited, he dialed his attorney's number again. When his assistant picked up—again—she seemed just as annoyed to hear Wes's voice as he was to hear hers. She explained—again—the D.A.'s office was working as quickly as possible to expedite his hearing so the Vegas charges could be settled and his monitoring device removed. She added it was important to wait for a judge who would go along with the D.A.'s sentencing recommendation, and his attorney was only looking out for his best interests. And to please stop calling.

Wes ended the call, then muttered a few choice expletives. But at least the urge to down a bag of oxy had passed. Mouse would never realize what a lifesaver his burger intervention had been.

Or maybe the man did know.

He only wished his father was as intuitive.

"Hi, Wes."

He turned to see Coop, dressed in jeans, collared shirt and white lab coat striding toward him with a big brotherly smile. "Hi, Coop."

"I'm excited you're going to do your community service at the morgue. I'm short-handed, and I sure can use someone like you to help out around here."

Wes tried to rally. "Yeah... good."

Coop's mouth tightened. "Any news about Meg?"

He didn't trust himself to speak, so he just shook his head.

"Okay, well, hang in there. I'm hoping for good news, like everyone else." Coop clapped him on the shoulder. "Let's go on up and I'll show you where you'll be working. This shouldn't take long."

They rode the elevator to a higher level floor, then walked out into an environment of metal and other non-porous materials. The temperature was just above freezing. Wes shivered.

"You'll get used to the cold," Coop offered. "And the lab coat helps."

Wes turned his head. "I'll get to wear a lab coat?"

"Of course."

Wes's chest expanded. Wait til Meg saw him in a lab coat. Then he remembered, and his chest deflated.

"These are the autopsy bays," Coop said, gesturing to a bank of stainless-clad rooms. "You'll be spending most of your time here and in the body storage rooms."

Coop walked toward a young dark-haired man with thick black eyebrows. A memory cord pinged in the back of Wes's mind.

"Wes, I believe you worked with Kendall Abrams before."

Right—the hayseed nephew of the former M.E. Dr. Bruce Abrams. "Yeah... hey, man."

"Hiya, Wes. How's it hangin'?"

"Um... fine." He remembered Kendall being a nice enough guy, but a little intense and not the sharpest pencil in the box. "So you changed your mind about working for the morgue?" He'd left to go back to removing roadkill for the Department of Transportation.

"Yep. I hope you don't hold it against me that my uncle turned out to be a serial killer. I don't think it runs in the family."

Wes glanced at Coop, who pulled his hand over his mouth.

"That's good," Wes offered. "Are you still studying forensics pathology?"

"Yep. I'm repeating my first year and it's much easier this time."

Coop coughed. "Kendall will be doing a work study, and Wes will be here for commun—" He stopped himself. "For a work study as well. The two of you will be deniers."

"What's that?" Kendall asked.

"You'll be responsible for handling and cleaning the bodies, and preparing them for autopsy."

Kendall grinned. "Do we get to watch the autopsies?"

Wes stared. The guy was still inappropriate.

"Unless there are other tasks that need to be done." Then Coop adopted a serious expression. "I can't stress enough how important it will be that you both practice good hygiene, and that you watch your intake of alcohol and... pharmaceuticals. You'll have to pass a drug test before you start, and random tests aren't out of the question."

Now Wes knew why E. wanted him to see Coop. He was *so* glad he hadn't made that trip to Little Five Points the previous night.

"Jeans and tennis shoes are fine as long as they're clean and decent," Coop said. "Golf shirts are fine, but no T-shirts. No shorts, no sandals, no smoking, no gum."

"How about snuff?" Kendall asked.

"Only on your break."

"Chew?"

"Same."

"Dip?"

Coop pursed his mouth. "Same. We'll go over this all again before you start. Any questions?"

Kendall raised his hand.

Coop smiled briefly. "Yes?"

"Will we be taking pictures of the bodies?"

Wes averted his gaze—the guy looked way too happy at the prospect.

Coop looked as if he thought so too. "Typically the medical examiner will handle the documentation photography. Any other questions?" He looked back and forth between them. "No? Okay, I'll be in touch soon with a date and time for your drug test. Be sure to stop by the admin office for the paperwork you'll need to fill out."

Wes let Kendall walk away, then he turned back to Coop. "I appreciate that you're letting me work here, but you should know that when I get this ankle bracelet removed, I'm going to Ireland to look for Meg, so I might be gone for a while."

Coop crossed his arms. "Do you think that's a good idea? I'm sure the police are doing everything they can, Wes."

He frowned. "What if Carlotta was missing?"

Coop sighed, then nodded. "You're right. I'd move heaven and earth to get there."

"Plus that asscrack friend of her dead brother's is over there doing nothing but brown-nosing Meg's dad. He's angling for an opportunity with Meg once she's found, I just know it."

"That doesn't matter if Meg loves you."

Wes scoffed. "It matters if he's there and I'm not... and it seems like he's *always* around, you know what I mean?"

The twitch of Coop's mouth said he knew alright. "Then you need to do what you need to do."

CHAPTER 14

Hi John, my name is Sarah. Tell me something about yourself, Carlotta texted.

How did you get my number?

From a friend who thought I would like you. What do you do for a living?

I'm independently wealthy, made my money in tech.

At the sound of the doorbell, Carlotta set her phone on her desk, thinking Valerie and Prissy must be early. When she glanced out the side window and saw Coop, she grinned and opened the door. "Hey, you."

"Hey, you," he said, holding up a carton of coffees. "Time for a latte?"

"You bet, come on in."

He stepped inside. "Should I have called?"

Carlotta took in his anxious expression and felt a little pang at his uncertainty. "No. Come by any time, day or night."

He grinned. "Day *or* night, huh?"

She laughed, glad to see his teasing side again, then stretched up for a deep, wet kiss.

"Mmm," he said. "What do I get if I bring donuts next time?"

"You'll have to try and see what happens. Hey, you're wearing the new tie." The one she'd bought him during the shopping trip with Jack.

He picked up the end. "Yeah... because my girlfriend bought it for me."

The word "girlfriend" triggered a strange reaction in her chest... which was crazy, because hadn't she referred to Coop as her boyfriend to Mrs. Winningham?

Coop glanced toward the kitchen. "Is Wes around? I brought him a coffee, too."

"No, he's at the driving range, pretending to like it. But it's better than hiding out in his room listening to sad music."

"No news about Meg, then?"

"Nothing, and I know it's killing him."

"Yeah, I could tell yesterday when he stopped by the morgue he had a lot on his mind."

She smiled. "Have I thanked you for arranging for him to work there?"

"Not today."

She laughed. "Well, thank you. It's the only thing he's been excited about lately. Aside from Meg, of course."

"I'll be happy to have him. The other young guy we're bringing in is Bruce Abrams's nephew, do you remember him?"

She squinted. "Dark hair, kind of weird?"

"That's him. He worries me a little, so it'll be nice to have Wes to rely on."

Coop nodded. "What are you into this morning?"

"Working in my office. By the way, Mom and Prissy are coming by in a bit. Prissy wants to see my office. They'll be happy to see you."

"I'll be happy to see them, too. How is your mom?"

"She seems to be doing great. I would say that she's like her old self, but honestly, I think she's better. She was drinking a lot back then, before they left." Another reason why she might've put the locket under the Christmas tree—she hadn't been thinking straight.

"It's pretty."

"Hm?"

He nodded to the locket she was rubbing between her thumb and finger. "I notice you wear it often. It suits you."

"Thanks," she murmured. "My mother gave it to me."

"Does it have any pictures inside?"

88

"Um... not yet." She reached for the latte and took a sip. "Mm, thank you."

"What are you working on?"

Glad for the change of subject, she smiled. "Come on back and I'll show you."

As they walked down the hallway, he glanced all around. "The renovations look great."

"All thanks to Wes—and Randolph. It's hard to remember how it looked before."

"I remember how your bedroom looked before," he teased. "Has Wes's snake gotten out lately?"

"No, thank goodness." She blushed, remembering how Coop had saved her when Einstein, Wes's black and gray spotted python had escaped and made its way into her bed. "I'm sure I was quite a sight standing on my dresser in my pajamas."

"Pale blue."

"Hm?"

"You were wearing a pale blue lace top thingy and a matching thong."

"You remember?"

He groaned. "Until the day I die."

She laughed again, enjoying his easy flirtation. Unlike Jack—

Carlotta stopped herself. She had to get out of the habit of comparing the two men.

"Uh-oh. Your face just went all weird. Did I say something wrong?"

There was his anxiety again. And why not? She hadn't given him reason to feel secure. She opened her mouth to reassure him, to tell him she loved him. "Coop, I...."

"What?"

Her mind raced, then she gestured toward the easel sitting in her office. "I'd like you to see the vision board for my business."

He stepped closer to the board covered with colorful images and words cut from magazines, newspapers, and books. "I've heard of this... you collage pictures to plan your strategy?"

She clasped her hands behind her back. "You probably think it's silly."

"Not at all. But what am I looking at here?"

She took a deep breath. "I'd like to build an online fashion business that revolves around personal shopping and brand representation."

He squinted. "Brand representation?"

"I would go to events wearing clothes that sponsors would pay me to wear." As soon as the words left her mouth, she wanted them back. He would think she was delusional. And frivolous. "What do you think?"

He turned to look her up and down. "I think anyone would pay big bucks to have that body represent them."

On her desk her phone vibrated—a text from John Smythe? Coop was standing close enough to see the screen, so she dove for it. She turned it over, smiling. "It's just Hannah, asking if we have a pickup today."

"You can text her back no," he offered.

"I'll do it later," she said, then slipped the phone into a drawer.

Then she walked over and looped her arms around his neck. "You were saying something about my body?"

He lowered his mouth to hers for a slow, exploratory kiss. She melted into him, kneading his back muscles. He pulled her sex against his hardening bulge and groaned into her mouth. "I want you."

"I want you, too," she breathed.

His mouth and hands became more insistent, fueling her own desire. Just as he slipped his hands under her blouse, the doorbell rang, cutting into their moment.

She pulled back and winced. "That would be Mom and Prissy."

He nodded, then puffed out his cheeks in an exhale. "I'll need a minute here."

She laughed, then headed to the front door to find Prissy pressing her face against the side window. "Let us in."

Carlotta opened the door and Prissy bounded inside. "Whose pretty car is that?" she asked, pointing to the vintage Corvette sitting in the driveway.

"It belongs to Mr. Coop. He brought me coffee. And he's looking forward to seeing you both." Valerie stood on the stoop, wearing a beige shirtdress and looking tentative.

"Hello, dear."

"Hi, Mom. Come in."

Valerie gave her a quick hug. Carlotta could still feel the resistance between them, but acknowledged it was mostly on her side.

"Where's your office?" Prissy asked.

Carlotta pointed down the hallway and Prissy skipped ahead of them.

"I see we came at a bad time," Valerie said, nodding to Carlotta's clothes.

She looked down to see her blouse was untucked from her skirt. She flushed and tucked it back in. "Sorry."

"Don't apologize," Valerie said with a little laugh. "You know I love Coop." She angled her head. "I hope you do, too."

Thankfully, her mother didn't wait for her to answer, just proceeded down the hallway. Carlotta followed her and found Coop entertaining Prissy with a magic trick, making quarters appear in the pockets of her dress.

"This is enough for ice cream," Prissy said, counting the coins. "Will you take me sometime?"

"Of course," Coop said.

"We'll double date. Carlotta and you, and me and Mr. Jack."

Coop's smiled dropped for only an instant. "I'm sure Jack would like that." He straightened to accept a warm hug from Valerie. Carlotta's heart expanded to see how Coop interacted with her family. He was so... perfectly... perfect.

"I'm going to leave and let you ladies visit," he said, stopping to plant a quick kiss on Carlotta's cheek.

"Thanks for the coffee," she murmured.

"You're welcome. Tell Hannah I said hello." His tone was easy, but it made her think he knew she hadn't been texting with Hannah.

Carlotta swallowed hard, then nodded.

"I like your office," Prissy said, pulling her attention back.

"Thank you, I like it, too." She gave her mother an appreciative smile. "You and Wes pulled this off right under my nose."

"Only because you were putting in so many hours at Neiman's to get the bridal salon going. Do you miss it?"

"Sometimes," Carlotta admitted. "But it was time to go."

"What's this?" Prissy asked, pointing to the vision board.

She explained what she had in mind for building a freelance business, then sighed. "But I'm kind of making this up as I go along."

"I see you're doing your research," Valerie said, picking up one of the many business books scattered on her desk.

"I still have a lot to learn."

"You'll get there," Valerie said, sounding more confident than Carlotta felt.

"Will you take pictures of me in my outfits to put on your blog?" Prissy asked.

"Absolutely... as soon I learn how."

"I'll show you how. It's easy."

Carlotta laughed, then remembered her sister had shown her how to use the camera on her phone. "I'll take you up on that."

"We can be partners," Prissy said.

"Carlotta," Valerie said from across the room, "what is this?"

Carlotta walked to the area she was staging to photograph outfits. Her mother was inspecting the mannequin-size hanger that a skirt, blouse and jacket were displayed on. "That's something I cobbled together. The top is a suit hanger with a twelve-inch drop. To the bottom I attached a skirt hanger with clips, and fashioned a head and flexible arms out of covered wire. It's easier to change outfits than on a mannequin, and the arms can be positioned at different angles."

"You made this?" Valerie asked.

Carlotta nodded.

"I want one!" Prissy announced. "Can you make one my size?"

"Then she could put together her own outfits," Valerie said and gave Prissy a pointed look. "Without changing a dozen times."

"Sure, we'll make one together," Carlotta promised.

Valerie was still inspecting the way it was constructed. "I'll bet you could mass produce these to sell."

Carlotta gave a little laugh. "I wouldn't know where to start."

"So let me."

Carlotta blinked. "You'd want to do that?"

"Sure. I still have contacts. I could make a few phone calls."

She'd never thought about her mom in any capacity other than social wife and mother. "That would be great, Mom."

Valerie winked at Prissy. "Maybe we'll all be partners." Then she glanced at her watch. "We need to go if we're going to make your dance rehearsal."

"Okay," Prissy said. "Can we come back sometime?"

Carlotta straightened one of the bows in her sister's dark hair. "Of course. You have to teach me everything you know about blogging and social media."

"That could take a while," Prissy said soberly.

Valerie exchanged wry glances with Carlotta, then said, "Can I take the hanger with me?"

"Sure. I'll carry it to your car."

She undressed the hanger, then removed it from the hook it was suspended from and followed them outside to the car. Just to see her mother driving was a miracle, but to see Valerie take an avid interest in things was a windfall.

That said, she needed to broach the subject still wedged between them. So after the hanger was stowed and Prissy was settled in the car and out of earshot, Carlotta said, "Mom, we need to talk."

Valerie's eyes turned troubled. "Okay... talk."

She chose her words carefully. "I know I said I don't want to know who my real father is... but I do have some questions."

Her mother hesitated, then assented with a nod.

"Did you love my father?"

Valerie flashed a little smile. "I thought I did, but we were so wrong for each other. Thankfully I came to that conclusion before I realized I was pregnant."

"Did he know you were pregnant?"

She shook her head. "By that time I'd met Randolph and was already half in love with him. When I told him about the baby, he said it didn't matter, that we'd get married and he'd raise it as if it was his own." She smiled. "And he did."

Carlotta couldn't argue that point. "Does Randolph know who he is?"

"Not that I know of."

"But if you didn't tell him, how could he know?"

Valerie looked anxious. "Because I don't know what I might've said when I was... unwell."

Carlotta hadn't considered that point. When she'd found her mother in Vegas after Randolph was arrested, she'd been almost child-like with huge memory gaps. "I understand, Mom. Thanks for answering my questions."

Valerie reached forward to clasp Carlotta's hand. "I'm glad you decided to let this go, darling. It's better for so many people."

Carlotta conjured up a smile and nodded.

CHAPTER 15

I'D LIKE to see a picture of you, Carlotta texted.

Send me one of you first

"What should I tell him?" Carlotta asked Hannah. They were sitting in the van outside a nursing home, waiting until the specified time to pick up the deceased.

"Tell him you want a dick pic."

"Ew."

"We rehydrated semen that could belong to this guy and you're gettting icked out over a photo?"

"Good point."

Send me a naughty pic—

"Oh, Christ," Hannah said, grabbing the phone before she could send the text. She deleted Carlotta's words, then punched in *Send me a picture of your big dick bad boy* and hit send. "There."

"What if we scare him off?"

Her phone vibrated and Hannah smirked. She held up the picture, an extreme closeup of an extremely excited penis. "Boom."

"Well, a lot of good that does. We can't tell the guy's race from his penis."

"I could if the lighting was better," Hannah murmured. "But yeah, let's ask to see his face."

Ooh, nice. Is your face that gorgeous, too?

What's the name of your friend who gave you my number?

"What should we say?" Carlotta asked.

"Since this guy uses John Smythe, let's use a common name, too."

Jane gave me your number, said you are hot

They waited for a response, but the minutes ticked by.

"We should go in," Carlotta said, nodding to the entrance.

"Ugh," I hate this, Hannah said. "It's so depressing to be around old people who are dying."

"As opposed to being around young people who are dying?"

She sighed. "You know what I mean. I think Coop is doing this on purpose."

Carlotta frowned. "Why would you say that?"

"I think he's keeping you away from crime scenes, because he doesn't want you going all Nancy Drew on him, and he doesn't want you crossing paths with Jack."

She scoffed. "Coop doesn't have to worry about me and Jack."

"So you told Coop that you love him?"

"Not... yet."

"Uh huh," Hannah said. She belched loudly, the third time in the space of a few minutes. "Sorry," she said. "It was something I ate."

Carlotta didn't comment, but from the weight Hannah had put on recently, it seemed as if she was eating not just *some*thing, but *every*thing.

Carlotta's phone rang and Hannah was still holding it. When "Fulton County Correctional Facility" flashed on the screen, she handed it back. "It's the third man in your love tripod."

Carlotta stuck her tongue out at Hannah, then connected the call. "Hello."

"This is a call from Inmate Peter Ashford," an automated voice said. "To accept the call, press one. To decline the call, press two." She pressed one.

"Carly?"

Her smile was involuntary, she realized, a reflex to his voice. "Hi, Peter. How are you?"

"I'm good," he said, and to her relief, his voice sounded strong and upbeat. "The guard told me you visited last week. I'm so sorry I didn't get to see you. I would've called sooner, but my phone privileges were suspended until today."

"The guard said there was an altercation?"

"Just a scuffle, I wasn't hurt."

"Are you ready for your bond review hearing?"

"I am, and I'm feeling pretty good about it. Of course, I'd feel better if Walt Tully was apprehended."

"Jack's working on his case," she said. "He asked Randolph if he knew where he might be. It sounds as if they've cast a wide net."

"I doubt if Walt went far," Peter said. "And I doubt if he's in his right mind."

"Why do you say that?"

"He was getting pretty paranoid when I was in Vegas communicating with him, trying to get him to go to the police. And remember when he took that alleged overdose?"

"When Randolph was first arrested," she said.

"Right. If he's still alive, he's probably not thinking straight."

Carlotta wet her lips. "Peter, the last time I visited, *you* said some pretty strange things."

"About what?"

"You said Randolph had a secret, and even my mother didn't know."

"I said that?"

"You don't remember?"

"Gosh, Carly, I must've been sleep deprived. Sorry if I worried you."

She smiled. "It's okay."

"Listen, I'm being told to wrap it up. I know this is a lot to ask, but will you be there for the bail hearing? My attorney says it would look good if the judge sees I have supporters."

"Hannah and I both will be at the bail hearing," she said, smiling at Hannah.

Hannah threw her a withering look.

"Thanks, Carly. I hope we can have coffee or a drink when I get out. I'd like to talk to you about some things."

"That sounds good, Peter. I'll see you soon."

"I still love you," he said. "I'll always love you."

But he saved her from an awkward response by ending the call.

Carlotta sighed. "At least he sounds better, more like himself."

Hannah belched. "What was all that about Randolph keeping a secret?"

"I think maybe he was trying to tell me Randolph isn't my father, although I don't know how Peter would know that. Or maybe he thought Randolph was having an affair with that realtor—I certainly did. Anyway, he was talking a little out of his mind that day, so it could be nothing."

"And when is this bail hearing I'm supposed to attend?"

"The day after tomorrow. It would mean a lot to me."

Hannah rolled her eyes. "Okay."

Carlotta phone buzzed. "It's from John—he sent a picture."

Hannah crowded in to see the selfie, then she gave a dry laugh. "He's a *kid*. Granted, a really cute Asian kid, but he's a kid."

Carlotta gaped, then texted *How old are you?*

15 Jane is in my biology class, do you go to our school?

"Holy cow," Carlotta said. "No wonder Patricia was down in the dumps after she met him. She must've felt like a fool. At least we can strike him from our suspect list."

"Not necessarily," Hannah said. "Don't underestimate the raging hormones of a fifteen-year-old. He might've followed her back to the hotel and things got nasty."

"And we would know if we could get our hands on the hotel security tapes."

Hannah sighed. "Working on it."

Carlotta raised her eyebrows. "I do believe you're starting to think I could be right about Patricia being murdered."

"I didn't say that, I'm just being a sounding board." She belched again, then pounded her breastbone.

Carlotta wrinkled her nose and waved her hand in the air. "Jesus, Hannah."

"Hey, that still smells better than this nursing home will. Come on, let's go bag an old bag."

CHAPTER 16

"I THOUGHT maybe practicing with Jade would help to take your mind off... things," Randolph said.

Wes sat in the passenger seat, watching a half-dead bug on the windshield of his father's vehicle flap around. He knew how the insect felt. And for the record, he didn't want to take his mind off Meg. He wanted to remember every pore on her sunny face, in case he never saw it again.

Randolph grunted, obviously bored with the silence. "Although how you're going to handle cards with your hands in such bad shape, I don't know."

Wes stared down at his bandaged fingers. "I think my attorney has blocked my calls. Have you talked to him lately?"

"Like I told you a dozen times, he's working on getting your hearing moved up, but the courts are jammed. And he does have other clients."

"I'll work it off. Whatever you have to pay him to make this happen, I'll work it off and pay you back."

"It's not about the money, Wes. These are federal charges. There are lots of moving parts, a lot of paperwork to coordinate with the Vegas district attorney." He sighed. "We've been over this."

"You think she's dead, don't you?"

Randolph shifted in his seat. "Let's don't go there. You have to believe she's okay."

"That she ran off with some guy on her own volition? She wouldn't do that."

"Okay," Randolph said calmly. "Then you'll just have to be patient until you hear from her father."

"Dr. Vincent won't take my calls, and neither will that asshat Mark. Jack Terry just puts me on ice. No one will tell me what the hell is going on!"

"Because," Randolph said in a voice reserved for toddlers, "there's nothing to tell. And maybe in this case, no news is good news."

The half-dead bug blew away. "I need to get over there."

"You know that's not possible."

"Maybe I'll just cut off my ankle bracelet."

"Don't even think about that. Besides, even if the ankle monitor comes off, you can't get a passport until the federal charges are settled, period."

"Can't you call in any favors? Surely the D.A.'s office owes you something for bringing down Mashburn & Tully?"

"I *have* called in favors. You have no idea—" Randolph wiped his hand over his mouth, then heaved a heavy sigh. "Look, Wes, I know it's hard, but you have to wait and let this play out."

He seethed. "You don't know anything about how I feel."

"I don't know anything about being away from someone I care about?" Randolph asked. "What do you think it was like being away from you and your sister for ten years?"

"I think we got the short end of that stick, don't you?"

A vein popped out in Randolph's temple. "You're right. And I would make it up to you both if I could."

Wes chewed on his cheek until he tasted blood, mad at himself for not telling Meg he didn't want her to go to Germany in the first place, mad at his Dad for being so smug, mad at the world for kicking him in the face every time he tried to be happy, goddammit.

"She's selling the car," he blurted.

Randolph turned his head. "What?"

"Carlotta... she's having Coop repair the Miata so she can sell it."

At the flash of pain in his dad's eyes, he almost felt bad... almost.

"It's her car... she can do with it whatever she thinks is best."

Randolph slowed the SUV, then turned into the parking lot of a night club. It was closed during the day, but Jade, a beautiful young card player who'd crushed him in a tournament, practiced card skills at a table in the bar. His father had hired her to coach Wes so he could advance to a higher level tier of Texas Hold 'em Poker.

Little did he know, Jade had revealed the reason she'd beat him—she'd cheated. And she'd offered to teach Wes how to cheat too. He just wasn't good at it yet.

Randolph pulled into a parking spot, then turned off the engine.

Wes frowned. "Are you staying?"

"Thought I might, to see how you've progressed."

As if he wasn't already miserable enough, now he had to play under his dad's microscope. He dragged himself out of the SUV, then slammed the door and plodded to a side entrance that led into the bar.

When he stepped inside the dark, cool interior, he felt his parasympathetic nervous system slow down. The chronic sleeplessness made his eyeballs ache, so he suffered both in the sun and in artificial light. He blinked to dispel the haloes around everything, then took a tentative step forward. A man behind the bar was wiping down a long mirror. He threw up his hand. They followed the sound of the *whoosh* and *thack, thack, thack* of cards being shuffled and split to a rear table.

Jade was an ethereal looking Japanese woman with a waterfall of white hair and black eyes. She was knock-out gorgeous, which she used to her advantage at the poker table. She'd certainly befuddled him when they'd played. Her hands moved like lightning. She lifted her gaze to him without missing a beat with the cards. "You don't look well."

"Rough couple of weeks," he muttered as he sat down.

"What happened to your hands?"

"Stuck them in a tank of piranhas."

She glanced up to Randolph, who stood nearby.

"Dad wants to see how much I've improved," Wes offered.

She blinked, meaning she understood his cheating education would have to wait for another day.

Randolph sat at the next table where he could observe.

Jade opened a case and pulled out a stack of chips for each of them. She dealt the cards for the first game, warily eyeing Wes throughout.

He played like a rube. His brain was gluey and his eyes felt like heavy rugs. He missed bets and misread cards and with his bandaged fingers, he might as well have been wearing boxing gloves. He dropped cards and generally made a mess of things. Worse, he could feel anger emanating from Jade.

He was making her look bad.

In the middle of the third game, she threw down her cards, then looked at Randolph. "You're wasting your money. He doesn't want to be here and he's not paying attention. Look at him—he's a mess. I have better things to do with my time."

"So play me instead," Randolph said, moving to their table.

Wes blinked in surprise.

Jade gave a little shrug, then moved Wes's smaller pile of chips to Randolph. She started to even up their two piles, then Randolph said, "I don't mind starting down a few hundred."

She gave another shrug, then dealt the first hand.

As players and as dealers, they were evenly matched. Wes silently rooted for Jade, but to his dismay, even with fewer chips, Randolph slowly got the upper hand on her. By the fifth hand, she was in danger of going out. His dad must've felt good about his hand because he went all in, forcing Jade to do the same. But when they revealed their cards, she beat his three queens with three kings.

She smiled, and reached forward to rake the pot toward her until Randolph put out his hand to stop her.

"What are you doing?" she asked.

He reached across the table to pick up the community king card, then turned it over and held it at an angle to the light. Then he looked up and made a rueful noise. "If you're going to cheat, don't play with someone who knows better. Either that, or learn how to be a better cheat."

Jade's mouth tightened, but she only sat back in her chair and crossed her arms.

"Let's go, Wes." Randolph stood and strode toward the door.

Wes stared wide-eyed at Jade and she gave him a sullen look.

"You told him?"

"Of course not."

"Right," she said, then looked away. "Get lost."

Wes caught up with his dad in the parking lot. "How did you know she cheated?"

"I saw her mark the card with her ring when she was dealing. She did the same thing when she played you in the tournament."

"Wait—you knew she cheated when she beat me in the tournament?"

"Sure did." Randolph planted his hands on his hips. "Son, everyone who plays cards knows how to cheat. And the best players know how to spot cheaters. Remember that. It's not worth it. If you're caught, you'll be blacklisted."

Wes was incredulous. "If you knew she cheated to beat me, why did you want her to coach me?"

"Because she has good hands for the game. And you've got something she doesn't—a great memory for cards. I hoped she would teach you a few good things along with the bad."

"She did," Wes said. "I was just off tonight."

"No, you're done with her. She doesn't know how to read players. If she did, she wouldn't have tried to cheat *me*."

Wes frowned. "So it was okay for her to cheat me, but not to cheat you?"

"Something like that."

Wes gave a little laugh. "You are unbelievable."

"I'm just trying to look out for you, son."

"If you were looking out for me, you'd help me get to Meg."

Randolph pressed his lips together. "Don't start this again."

Wes turned in the opposite direction. "I'll walk home."

"Wes," his dad called, "don't do that. It's a long way."

"Yeah," he shouted over his shoulder, "well, maybe it'll help to take my mind off... things."

CHAPTER 17

VALERIE'S FACE shone with excitement. "I talked to an attorney about the steps to getting a patent on your invention."

Carlotta blinked. "My invention?"

"That's what it is," her mother said, gesturing to the hanger she'd brought back. "You created it... you invented it."

"I... guess so," she agreed.

"We need to think of a good name for it." Her mother pushed a sheet of paper across Carlotta's desk. "I took the liberty of jotting down a few ideas, but of course it's up to you."

Carlotta tamped down her surprise, then glanced over the list.

"I think you should call it the Style Me Hanger," Prissy offered.

"That's a good name," Carlotta said. "All of these are good."

"And I spoke with a local fabricator," Valerie said. "He can use your model to create a prototype, and once we approve it, he can manufacture as many as we need."

Her smile felt tremulous. "As many as we need?"

"Well, at first just for sales demos and trade shows. But once we get our own website up and marketing in place, I think we'll sell thousands."

"Th-thousands?"

"And if we can get on one of the home shopping networks, tens of thousands."

Carlotta's eyes widened. "Tens of thousands?"

"Sweetheart, I think this is a terrific product that women will want in their closets, more than one, in fact. There's nothing like it on the market."

"She's right," Prissy offered. "I taught Mom how to search and we looked for *hours*."

"And if we can sell the hangers into boutiques and department stores," Valerie added, "who knows how big the business could become."

"You have to make one for pre-teens, too," Prissy said, as if it was a foregone conclusion.

"And why not a male version?" Valerie added.

Carlotta sat back in her chair, slightly in awe. "You've put a lot of thought into this."

Valerie's face blanched. "Have I overstepped?"

She laughed. "Not at all. I'm so impressed. I've never seen this side of you."

Her mom smiled, then lifted her chin. "And do you like it?"

"I do," she said, nodding. "Very much." Then she winced. "But this kind of undertaking could be expensive."

"I know," Valerie said, her voice laced with concern. "That's why we need to incorporate as soon as possible."

Carlotta's eyebrows climbed. "Incorporate?"

"You should consider a pass-through S-Corporation," Prissy said solemnly.

"But Mom, I don't have the money to fund this project, not yet anyway."

"Your dad and I will fund it. It could be a family business. We'll all have roles."

Family. Her mother was positively glowing. "And what does Randolph think about it?"

"Your father thinks it has potential," she said lightly.

"He said it sounded girly," Prissy offered. "Then Mom said his driving range was his pet project, and this would be hers. Then they kissed a bunch and he handed her the checkbook."

Valerie smiled. "It did go something like that. Anyway, I have a tidy sum to tap into for seed money, enough to get us up and running, I believe."

Carlotta laughed, then lifted her hands. "Okay, if that's what you want to do, I'm on board."

"Me too," Prissy said. "I'll be the brand ambassador for kids my age."

Carlotta looked back and forth between the female dynamos. "I can see I have my work cut out for me to keep up with you two."

Valerie stood. "Prissy, we have to go. Carlotta, I'll call you about availability before I reach out to an attorney about setting up the business. Be thinking of a name for your hanger."

"I will," Carlotta said, her head spinning. She pushed to her feet to walk them out. At the door, she embraced her mother, and felt a small break in the ice between them. Maybe this project would be good for them, to spend more time together. But when she pulled back, her mother's gaze landed on the locket, and her eyes clouded.

"Mom—" Carlotta began.

"Jack!" Prissy shouted, then shot out the door.

Carlotta turned to see Jack climbing out of his sedan. She realized he was wearing some of his new clothes and she conceded she'd done an exceptional job. Jack was a breathtakingly good-looking man, even more so in the right clothes for his big body. He stopped and squatted down to say hello to Prissy and to tug on her pigtail. And he must've said something about her dress because she grinned and did a twirl. He laughed, and in that moment, Carlotta saw the side of him he rarely showed. It was special.

"Does he stop by often?" Valerie asked.

She turned her head and realized her mother had been watching her watch Jack. "Jack? No... not lately anyway."

"There was something between the two of you at one time?"

"There was something," she conceded. "But we didn't agree on what it was... or could be."

"And now there's Coop."

Carlotta smiled. "Yes. Now there's Coop."

"We'll go and leave you to your visitor," Valerie said, then opened the door.

Carlotta stepped out onto the stoop and waited while Jack greeted her mother and said goodbye to Prissy. Carlotta waved as they pulled out of the driveway, then turned her attention to Jack. "What brings you here? You haven't been by in so long even Mrs.

Winningham asked about you the other day."

He climbed up on the stoop. "Carlotta…"

She could tell from the look on his face that something was very wrong. "Jack… what is it?"

"Let's go inside," he said, then stepped forward to open the door.

She followed him into the living room. He shut the door carefully—too carefully. "You're scaring me. Is it Meg? Do you have bad news?"

He turned to face her. "No, there's no news on Meg." He wet his lips. "It's Peter."

"He didn't get bail?" Then she frowned. "No, wait—his bail hearing isn't until tomorrow."

"Carlotta," Jack said in a choked voice. "Peter is dead."

She squinted. "What did you say?"

"Peter… is dead."

She gave a little laugh. "But that's impossible. I talked to him yesterday, and he was fine, better than he'd been in a long time. This is some kind of mistake, Jack."

His face gentled. "I wish it was. He was killed by another inmate about an hour ago."

She shook her head in denial, then her face crumpled as her sudden tears broke free. "No… no," she cried. She gasped for air, sobbing… her heart and lungs were on fire with pain.

Jack pulled her against his chest and tucked her head under his chin. "I'm sorry…. I'm so sorry this happened."

She clung to him, crying harder as the awfulness of his words sunk in. *Peter was dead.* It seemed incongruous that the beautiful blond man who had stolen her teenage heart was gone from this earth. Jack rocked her gently, taking the brunt of her weight. At length she quieted, but he still held her until the sound of another vehicle arriving pulled them apart.

She wiped her eyes with her palms, then accepted the handkerchief Jack offered to blot her tears and blow her nose. A few seconds later, Coop appeared at the door. She realized he of course would've gotten the call at the morgue. Jack walked to the door and let him in. Coop's gaze bounced between her and Jack and it was apparent where she'd taken refuge by the wet stain and streaks of mascara on Jack's shirt.

"I just heard," he said, crossing to Carlotta. "Are you okay?"

She shook her head no and a fresh wall of tears gathered to spill out. He pulled her into his arms and she pressed her face into his chest. He kissed her forehead. "I'm sorry you're sad," he murmured. "I wish I could take it away."

Jack cleared his throat. "I should leave."

Carlotta lifted her head and sniffed, wiping her face with his handkerchief. "Don't go, Jack. Tell me what happened to Peter."

Jack hesitated then sighed. "He was in the lavatory with some other inmates. I'm told a guard was nearby. No one heard or saw anything." He swallowed. "Apparently, he wasn't missed for some time, and during the search his body was discovered."

She covered her mouth to stem another wave of tears. "Do they know who did it? There must be cameras everywhere."

"Not in this particular area of the lavatory," Jack said. "And so far, if anyone knows anything, they're not talking."

She made a frustrated noise. "But how was he killed? Was he stabbed?"

Jack shifted, then glanced at Coop. "That'd be up to the M.E. to say."

"So there weren't any visible wounds on the body?" she asked.

Jack looked at Coop, then Coop sighed. "It appears at first glance that his neck was broken."

She shrank back. "Did he fall?"

"No," Jack said. "It was intentional."

"Peter was a big man," she said. "What kind of force would it take to break his neck?"

The men once again traded glances.

"A lot," Coop finally said.

"It's a very precise maneuver," Jack added.

"So... someone with training... a military background?"

Jack gave a half-nod. "Maybe."

But the men weren't telling her everything, she could tell. Then another possibility occurred to her. "A professional hit."

She could tell by Jack's body language that she'd landed on his theory.

"It's impossible to say," Coop offered.

"Someone wanted him dead?" she cried. "Who?" Then as

soon as she said it, a name slid into her brain. "Walt Tully."

"Carlotta, you don't know that," Jack said. "Don't speculate on why it happened, you might never get a satisfactory answer."

"But he's the person who stood to lose the most if Peter turned state's evidence and testified against him. When we were in Vegas, Peter was in constant contact with Walt. Jack, do you have any leads on Walt's whereabouts?"

His mouth twitched downward. "You know I can't share information about an ongoing investigation."

She started crying again, and Coop pulled her close.

Jack sighed. "I would if I could." His phone sounded from his belt. He glanced down, then said, "I need to go. Will you be okay? When will Wes be home?"

"I'll stay with her tonight," Coop said.

Jack's mouth rearranged into a flat smile. "Carlotta, my condolences."

She sniffed. "Thank you, Jack."

Jack's gaze bounced all around the smartly renovated living room and she wondered if he was remembering how many times he'd stayed there... the things they'd done. Everything was different now.

Everything.

He walked to the door, then nodded. "Coop."

"See you, Jack."

When he left, the door banged closed behind him.

CHAPTER 18

"Mmm," Carlotta murmured, snuggling back into the warmth behind her.

"Mmm," a man whispered in her ear.

In her fugue state, she tried to identify the voice. Jack? No. Peter? No... and why did it hurt when she thought of Peter? Coop?

"Yes?" he said.

Her eyes popped open. Sunlight streamed into her bedroom. Had she been speaking aloud? And why did her head feel so achy?

And then she remembered—Peter was dead.

The grief hit her anew and a solitary tear rolled down her cheek and onto her pillow. She sniffled.

"Are you wake?" Coop whispered.

"Yes," she croaked.

He folded his arm around her and clasped her hand. "I know you're hurting. I know you'll miss Peter."

She nodded against her pillow. "He was my first love."

"That's a big one," Coop agreed.

"He didn't deserve to die like that."

"No one does."

She rolled over to face him, then registered how oddly normal it seemed to find him in her bed. "Thanks for staying last night."

Coop smiled. "Any time."

Part of their pledge to take things slow meant no sleepovers.

But she realized she could get used to seeing him like this, without his glasses and sexily rumpled. "Hey, you."

He touched his forehead to hers. "Hey, you."

She put her hand on his bare chest and felt his heart beating below her palm. "For a man who makes his living with dead people, you're so alive."

"Working around death will drive you one way or the other," he said. "It's always made me appreciate life that much more." Then he dropped a kiss on her cheek. "Speaking of which, regrettably, I need to take off."

He climbed out of her bed and stretched high. She made a mournful sound of loss.

"You don't have to get up. Go back to sleep."

"I'm enjoying the view," she said, admiring his lean, tone body clad only in boxer briefs.

"Careful," he said, "I might climb back in there with you, and then I'd really be late."

She smiled. "Would that be so bad?"

He groaned. "No... but I don't want to have to rush."

Unlike Jack— She stopped herself.

"Right," she agreed.

"But wow, you're making this hard." He dropped his gaze to his boxers. "Literally."

She laughed softly while he picked up his jeans from a chair, then stepped into them. "Did you hear Wes come in last night?"

"Yeah, it was late," he said. "And he left already."

"Chance picks him up early to get to the driving range."

"I don't guess he's heard any news about Meg?" Coop asked.

"Jack said yesterday there've been no developments."

"Wow, that's rough. I keep hoping for the best."

"That's all we can do," she agreed.

While Coop pulled a shirt over his head, she pushed up to lean back against the pillows. "I assume you'll be performing the autopsy on Peter's body?" she asked quietly.

He found his glasses and put them on. "Probably not since he and I were acquainted."

"But you'll let me know the results?"

He shook his finger. "Don't put me in the middle of you and Jack." He frowned. "Any more than you already have."

She pouted.

He leaned down for a quick kiss. "Try to have a good day, okay?"

"Okay."

"Any plans?"

"I'll probably just take it easy around here, do some reading."

"Okay... I'll call you later."

She watched him leave her bedroom, thinking how casual and drama-free he was compared to— She stopped herself.

Carlotta listened until Coop's vehicle had left, then she pulled herself up to take a shower and pull on a loose shift dress. She looked puffy from all the crying but she applied extra makeup and added big sunglasses. While she walked to the Marta station, she checked her text messages.

Hey, Sarah, still waiting on a foxy picture

"Keep waiting, junior," she muttered.

Hi, Sis... really sorry to hear about Peter. He was good to me. Glad Coop stayed over.

She smiled, but her heart squeezed for Wes. He was probably feeling as if he might lose someone close to him, too.

Holy fuck, I just heard about Peter. Where are you?

Where are you?

Where the fuck are you?

Carlotta sighed, then punched in Hannah's number.

She answered on the first ring. "Holy crap, I got up this morning to get ready to go to Peter's bail hearing, then I hear on the news that he's *dead*. What the fuck happened?"

"He—" Carlotta broke off, then started again. "He was killed by another inmate."

"Wow, that's a bad way to go. How are you holding up?"

"I was a mess when Jack came by yesterday to tell me, but Coop stayed with me last night, and I'm better this morning."

"I'll bet you are."

"It's not like that. It was nice... he was sweet."

Hannah grunted disapproval. "It sounds like you're outside."

"I am. I'm heading downtown to run an errand. Can we talk later?"

"Sure. Since I don't have to go to the bail hearing, I can do some business this morning. If all goes well, I'll give you a private demonstration soon."

Carlotta made a face. "Can't wait."

"Listen, Carlotta... I know I gave you hell over Peter, but when push came to shove with Mashburn & Tully's Ponzi scheme, he tried to do the right thing, and I respect him for that."

She smiled into the phone. "Thanks, Hannah."

Carlotta ended the call, then hurried to catch the next southbound train. She got off at Little Five Points and a block before she reached the headquarters of the *Atlanta Journal-Constitution*, she stopped to pick up a box of Krispy Kreme donuts and two coffees. When she knocked on the door of Rainie Stevens's office, she smiled. "I come bearing gifts."

The curvy redhead gave her a deadpan look. "Gifts from you, Carlotta, always come with strings attached."

"You're so cynical." She opened the box of donuts to allow the scent of fried sugar and fat to waft out.

"I can't," Rainie said with a frown. "I'm dieting to get into my wedding gown." She lifted her left hand to show off her glittering rock.

"Wow, congratulations. Coop said you got engaged. To a dentist, I believe?"

"Yep. I got tired of waiting for Coop waiting for you. I hear you're together now?"

Carlotta nodded, then took a drink from the cup of coffee.

"Did Jack Terry withdraw his name?"

"That's not fair."

"Not to Coop," Rainie said pointedly. Then she sighed. "Okay, I might as well." She pulled a donut from the box, took a bite, and made a feel-good sound. "What do you want?" she asked thickly.

Carlotta leaned a hip on Rainie's desk. "Actually, I'm here to talk about another man—Peter Ashford."

"Jail murder?"

Carlotta swallowed hard, then nodded. "He was... a friend of mine. He worked at Mashburn &Tully with Randolph."

"Wait—didn't the two of you date?"

"Yes, on and off. But I ended it... before he went to jail."

"Can't blame you for that."

"But Peter didn't deserve to be murdered in the jail lavatory."

"Have they caught the inmate who did it?"

"Not yet. No cameras in that area. Rainie... someone broke his neck."

Rainie frowned. "That's not easy to do."

"I have it on authority it might've been a professional hit."

The woman leaned forward. "I'm listening."

"I was wondering if you have any confidential informants at the jail to find out if Peter was targeted by someone on the outside."

"Why do you suspect a conspiracy?"

"Because Peter was supposed to have a bail hearing today."

Rainie raised an eyebrow. "And Walter Tully is still on the run."

Carlotta nodded. "Will you make some inquiries?"

The reporter swallowed. "If you promise the next time you come around you bring something sugar-free."

"Deal," Carlotta said. "You still have my number?"

"Yes." She gave Carlotta a dry smile. "Memorized from how many times I saw it on Coop's phone when we were dating."

"Okay, then." She picked up her coffee to leave.

"Carlotta?"

She looked back.

"The man is nuts for you. Don't break his big heart."

Carlotta smiled. "I don't plan to."

CHAPTER 19

"IT'S A FULL house," Hannah said as they filed into the church.

"Peter's family is well-known," Carlotta said. "And Peter had lots of school friends and fraternity brothers."

"And let's face it, people love a society funeral."

"There's that, too," Carlotta agreed. Sadly, it was the same church where only a few weeks earlier, Patricia had been eulogized.

She thought she'd prepared herself, but when she saw the closed casket holding Peter's body in front of the altar, she felt light-headed.

"Easy," Hannah said. "Don't faint on me. Deep breaths. We're almost to a pew and you can sit down."

She forced air in and out of her lungs.

Hannah nodded to a pew on the right. "There's Coop. Oh, and Jack."

Sure enough, Jack was sitting next to Coop, both smartly dressed in dark suits. The men stood when they reached the pew to allow them to slide in, both instantly attentive.

"Hannah, sit by me," she murmured.

"I'll sit on the other side of Coop," Hannah whispered. "That way the guys can have a nice, juicy Carlotta sandwich."

Leave it to Hannah to find levity in any moment.

Jack and Coop parted for her to sit between them. "Are you okay?" the men asked at the same time, then looked at each other.

"I'm fine," she assured them. "I just want to get through the next hour."

A small murmur sounded from the rear. When she turned her head to see what had caused the stir, she recognized Senator Max Reeder from television. He and his wife were being escorted through the crowd to the Ashford family seating section.

"High connections," Coop observed.

"Publicity opportunity," Jack said.

Carlotta was riveted on Peter's parents, who looked stoic and drawn, and she realized with a start if she hadn't broken the engagement, she'd be sitting in the family section. She shuddered, overcome with the whiff of death, and felt guilty for sitting there, seemingly safe outside of its reach.

Coop reached for her right hand at the same time Jack clasped her left hand. Their hands were equally large and warm... but so different.

Among the crowd she recognized Tracey Tully Lowenstein and her husband Dr. Frederick Lowenstein. She briefly wondered if Tracey had purchased the pink lingerie she'd been considering that day at Neiman's.

She recognized other faces, acquaintances from the country club, people she'd known loosely most of her life but had come into contact with again when she'd started seeing Peter after his wife died.

A wad of emotion lodged in her throat. Not long ago she'd been so envious of Angela and Peter's life, had lain awake at night coursing with hurt and rejection, and now they were both gone. Life turned on a dime. She squeezed the hands of the men on either side of her, grateful to have people in her life who cared about her.

Music began to play, signaling the start of the service. For Carlotta, it was the start of a river of silent tears. She'd loved Peter for most of her life. His last words to her on the phone had been a profession of devotion.

I still love you... I'll always love you.

She recalled now that he was making plans for after he was released on bail. He'd wanted to meet for a drink, said he had things he wanted to talk to her about. At the time she'd dismissed it as a manufactured reason for them to get together... but now she wondered if there was something else he wanted to tell her... the alleged secret of Randolph's? Much of his conversation had been about his speculation on Walt Tully's state of mind.

Did Peter worry that Walt would have him quieted?

She tried to listen to the service, the eulogy, the memorialization, the music, but she was bound up in her own memories of Peter, the happy, reckless boy who'd climbed the tree outside her bedroom window to see her and help her sneak out at night to ride around and neck in his car. She felt a pang of loss for the optimistic, youthful people they'd been, still insulated from the sorrow life had waiting for them.

At the end of the service, the four of them joined the long receiving line to speak with Peter's parents. But when his mother caught sight of Carlotta, she froze. "You shouldn't be here," she said.

Peter's father tried to soothe his wife, but she pulled away. "You abandoned Peter when he needed you, and now look what's happened."

Around them, people were staring. Nearby, Max Reeder's reproachful gaze slid over her.

Carlotta endured the woman's verbal punishment wordlessly. Hadn't she been wrestling with the same thoughts herself? That somehow if she hadn't broken their engagement, he would still be alive?

Among the sea of faces around them, her attention snagged on one—Tracey Lowenstein. Surprisingly, the woman looked as if she felt sorry for Carlotta, then she averted her gaze. Or was she, perhaps, feeling guilty because she suspected her fugitive father had had a hand in Peter's death?

"Let's go," Coop murmured in her ear, then steered her away. "People say terrible things when they're grieving, don't take it to heart."

"She needed to lash out at someone," Jack added.

"Guess we won't be going to the graveside service," Hannah said wryly.

They all turned to look at her.

She frowned. "What? We were all thinking it."

When they walked outside, they congregated near the edge of the parking lot.

"I didn't see Wes," Coop said.

"I told him not to come," Carlotta said. "He has too much on his mind right now." She looked to Jack. "Any word about Meg?"

He shook his head and his expression looked dour. "If the police in Dublin don't get a break soon, they're going to close the case."

She groaned. "How can they do that?"

"I hate to say it, but this is why tourists can be a target for crime—there's so much ambiguity as to what happened, cases are difficult to investigate and to prosecute." Jack checked his phone, then frowned. "Sorry, I need to go."

"Me, too," Coop said.

"I can take you home," they said to Carlotta in unison, then glanced at each other.

"*I'll* take her home," Hannah said, trumping them both. "Come on, Carlotta."

CHAPTER 20

"YOU WERE right," Carlotta said to Dr. Denton. "I was operating on limiting beliefs about what I can and can't do. I made a list, and then I questioned everything on the list, and I have a new perspective."

He looked pleased. "I'm glad you found the exercise helpful. What have you decided to do?"

"I'm going to launch my own business. And I'm going to start trusting my instincts more."

"Good."

"If I'd done that when Patricia first died, I could've preserved more evidence from the crime scene."

Dr. Denton looked startled. "Excuse me?"

"Patricia—my coworker who died during our business trip to Dallas."

"Yes, you've mentioned her death as an inciting incident for leaving your job at Neiman Marcus."

"Yes, well, I didn't mention that even though the police ruled her death an accident, I believe she was murdered."

His eyes were wide. "By whom?"

"I have two suspects I'm honing in on. I'll have more to go on when the DNA test comes back."

"DNA test?"

"From the semen in the condom I found in her bathroom." She smiled. "You wanted me to realize that I have skills, and I do.

I'm good at this."

He shifted in his chair. "Carlotta, has it ever occurred to you that you might be fabricating mysteries where they don't exist as a way of avoiding solving the problems in your own life?"

She crossed her arms. "I don't fabricate mysteries... they are what they are."

"Yet you're the only one who believes there's a mystery in this instance."

"Maybe I'm the only one who cares."

He nodded. "So you think that by delving into Patricia's death, you're proving that you care more than anyone else?"

"I don't see it that way—I just happen to be in a position to help. I'm in possession of a lot of the puzzle pieces. It's my duty to do something about it. Just like with Peter's death."

He glanced at his notebook. "This is your former fiancé who was killed by a fellow inmate while he was in custody."

"Right. But I think it could've been a professional hit, and someone on the outside had it done."

His eyebrows climbed. "And do you have someone in mind for who could've orchestrated this professional hit?"

"Walter Tully."

He squinted. "Walter Tully, the former partner at Mashburn & Tully, the man who's on the run?"

"Yes. He's the one who had the most to lose if Peter made bail."

"I see. So you're investigating Peter's death as well?"

"I guess you could say that."

He made a few notes on his pad. "Okay, that's all the time we have. But I want you to think about what we talked about—if you're concocting mysteries to avoid facing some of the unknowns in your own life."

She smiled. "I will... but I'm not." She pushed to her feet and picked up her purse, then left his office feeling better than she had in a while.

There was something to this brainstorming problems with a psychologist.

On the way to the nearest train station she phoned Rainie and left a message asking if she had updates from her confidential sources. When she ended the call she remembered Rainie's parting advice about not breaking Coop's heart. Feeling inspired, she pulled up his text address, then searched for a heart emoji to send.

The she frowned—which one? The big red perfect heart, or the little pink heart? Or the beating heart? What did they all mean, and how would he perceive whatever symbol she sent?

She changed her mind, then boarded a train to Hannah's part of town. On the ride she listened to a podcast about online marketing. She understood only about half of it, but some of the terms and concepts were starting to sink in.

When she reached Hannah's apartment building, dread rolled in her stomach. Her friend had decided to give Carlotta a private demonstration of her new business, and she wasn't sure she wanted to see it. There were only so many things that could be done with a tripod in the bedroom.

Resigned, she climbed the stairs to Hannah's unit, then rang the bell. Hannah opened the door, vibrating with excitement and dressed in a peignoir from the 1960s... it was a nice color of aqua, but the skimpy robe would've fit her friend better ten pounds ago. It was impossible not to notice the recent rounding of her curves— of course Hannah could pull off any body shape with panache.

"Come in, come in," Hannah said, waving her inside. "Everything is set up in the bedroom. I've been waiting for you before I start."

Carlotta managed a shaky smile. "Okay." She followed Hannah down the hallway toward her bedroom. "Can you give me a hint so I'll know what to expect?"

"Okay." Hannah beamed. "I'm a mook banger!"

She squinted. "What's a mook... and why would you want to bang one... on camera?"

"A mukbanger," Hannah enunciated, then opened her bedroom door and gestured with much flourish to the lavish feast spread on the bed, picnic style.

Carlotta stared at the food—a roast of some kind slathered with sauce, bowls of mashed potatoes and other vegetables, a pan of cornbread, and a giant chocolate cake. "I don't get it. Are you bulimic?"

Hannah laughed. "No... my new business is called Hannah Eats." She gestured to her phone mounted on the tripod. "I eat food on camera."

She lifted one eyebrow. "Why?"

"People watch me—lots of them."

Carlotta lifted the other eyebrow. "*Why?*"

She shrugged. "It varies. Some people are lonely and want to share a virtual meal... some people are dieting and want to eat vicariously through me... some people fetishize food and want to rub one out while I butter a hot yeast roll."

She wrinkled her nose. "How many people?"

Hannah smiled. "I have a thousand subscribers."

"A thousand people watch you eat?"

"It's more of a performance, really. I describe the food down to the smallest detail, and make lots of yummy noises. And they don't just watch—they pay me to watch."

Carlotta gasped. "How much?"

"Each subscriber pays me a dollar a day."

"You make a thousand dollars a day *eating?*"

"Well, deduct the cost of the food, my costumes, and my equipment, but yeah, I'm a fucking genius." She gestured to a plate of food in the corner out of sight of the camera. "I made you a plate. Hurry, it's almost time to start."

Carlotta shook her head in wonder, but took her place. Her stomach growled at the aromas wafting off the comfort food. "This explains a lot," she said. "The belching, and—" She gave Hannah a pointed look. "The extra pounds."

Hannah gave a dismissive wave as she adjusted the camera, then reclined on the bed with a giant hunk of cornbread. "That's not because of the food... I'm pregnant."

CHAPTER 21

"HOW FAR along is she?" Wes asked Chance, then swung at the ball.

"About four months. Dude, I can't stop grinning. I mean, another me running around, can you imagine?"

"No. I mean—yeah, that's gonna be crazy, alright." Wes bent over to tee up another ball. "Congrats, man. It's nice to have some good news."

Chance sobered. "Still no word from Meg?"

"Nope." He channeled all his frustration into his swing. The ball sailed straight and high, arcing nicely before falling to significant yardage.

"Dude, that was nice. When did you get so good at smacking the ball?"

"Gotta smack something," he said, then leaned down to tee up again. From his belt his phone rang. As usual, his pulse spiked with hope, and when he saw Mark's name come up on the screen, he scrambled to connect the call. "Hello? Hello, Mark?"

"Hi, Wes. Yeah, it's me." His voice broke. "I've got news, but it's not good."

Wes's heart dropped to his ankles. "What?" he choked out.

"The local police and the embassy finally got a lead on Meg's disappearance."

"But that's good news, right?"

"They think she's been trafficked out of Ireland to another

country, maybe Russia."

His heart detonated. "Trafficked? You mean as in…?"

"Yeah," Mark said. "Her dad is like a wild man. We both feel so helpless."

"But if the police and the embassy know, they'll find her, right?"

"They said they'll look for her, but because of international jurisdictions and the history of this kind of thing happening before, they basically told us we need to prepare ourselves that we might never see her again."

"No!" Wes yelled into the phone. "I won't accept that!"

"I have to go, man. Dr. Vincent is losing his mind."

"Wait—" But he'd ended the call.

Rage and horror rose in his body to the point he thought he might have a stroke. He welcomed one—his brain was bound to explode anyway if Meg didn't come home. He picked up the driver and heaved it out over the grass, bellowing as he released it. It swung head over handle a dozen times before dropping in the distance.

"Dude, are you okay?" Chance asked.

"No," he bit out. "I'm about as far from okay as I could be!"

His father came out of the office—he'd obviously witnessed the meltdown on the tee box. Customers were gawking.

"Wes… come in here, please."

"Go to hell!" Wes shouted, then jogged to the parking lot where he could think. What to do… what to do…

He needed a fake passport. Once he got documentation to travel, he'd cut off his ankle monitor. He pulled out his phone, then scrolled until he found Mouse's number, then connected the call. He paced, willing the man to answer. "C'mon, Mouse… pick up… pick up."

"Wes," the man boomed. "What's going on, Little Man? Any news from your sweet Meg?"

"Yeah," he said. "It's not good, man. I gotta get over there, and I need a passport. Can you get me one?"

The man sighed heavily into the phone. "Uh, yeah, I have some contacts. Pretty pricey, though."

"How much?"

"Fifteen large."

Wes grimaced. "I'll get the money... somehow."

"Okay, but it's gonna take maybe four or five days."

That would give him time to scrape together the funds. "Okay, what do you need from me?"

"Text me a selfie wearing a decent shirt on a white background, then I'll be in touch when it's ready."

"Thanks, man." He ended the call, and blew out a long, hot breath. It felt good just to be doing something.

But now he needed cash—a lot of it. Enough for the documentation, a last-minute flight to Ireland, and expenses... maybe twenty-five grand. He walked back to the tee and yelled for Chance. "Dude... can I borrow your car?"

Chance fished his keys out of his pocket, then tossed them to him.

Randolph had been talking to customers, but now turned toward him. "Wes... where are you going?"

He didn't respond, just strode to Chance's car and climbed in. He'd lost his driver's license so long ago, sitting behind the wheel felt alien to him. But he fired up the engine and after adjusting the seat, headed south to the night club where Jade practiced cards. He parked, then jogged to the side door and into the bar.

The bartender looked up from sweeping and Wes gave him a quick wave, then loped to the rear of the bar, praying to find her. When he heard the sounds of her shuffling and stacking, he heaved a sigh of relief. He was so winded when he reached the table where she sat, he had to stop to get his breath.

She sat shuffling until he recovered, then rolled her big black eyes up to him. "What?"

"I need twenty-five grand."

She laughed. "Who doesn't?"

"In three days," he said. "Can you find a game? Maybe we can work together."

She was quiet for a while, then raised an eyebrow. "You mean, you're willing to play my way?"

"Yeah. We'll split our winnings, fifty-fifty."

"Sixty-forty. And if you get caught, you're on your own."

"Okay," he said. "What do I need to do?"

Jade nodded to the chair opposite her. "Sit. And get ready to concentrate."

CHAPTER 22

CARLOTTA WAS sitting at her desk, trying to concentrate on the book she was reading about social media, but she kept getting lost and rereading the same paragraphs over and over.

Feeling restless, she set the book aside and allowed her mind to wander to the things pressing in from the corners of her mind.

The DNA tests... her relationship with Coop... Meg's disappearance... Peter's death... Hannah's baby.

She smiled. That was the one bright spot of late. She laughed just thinking about Hannah as a mother and wondered if the tyke would come out wearing a dog collar.

Her phone rang and she reached for it. When she saw Rainie's name come up, she connected the call, crossing her fingers the woman had information. "Hi, Rainie. What's up?"

"Courtesy call," Rainie said. "My CI at the jail says the scuttlebutt is that Peter Ashford was targeted, like you said."

Carlotta closed her eyes against the ugliness of it... Peter caught unaware, then knowing he was going to die. She finally found her voice. "Targeted by whom?"

"There's a sense that it came from 'higher up,' but it could've been an inmate grudge or a gang initiation."

"So no one saw who did it?"

"If they did, they're not willing to come forward."

"Was Walt Tully's name mentioned?"

"Not that my CI had heard." Rainie sighed. "Look, Carlotta, I don't have the resources to investigate something like this. I passed the information I got to Jack Terry. Hopefully the police or the D.A.'s office have the time and energy."

Carlotta winced. "Did you happen to mention my name to Jack?"

"Uh…"

Her phone buzzed—it was Jack calling. She grimaced. "Later, Rainie. Thanks." Then she connected Jack's call. "Hi, Jack. What's up?"

"You know what's up," he said in an irritated voice. "I just got off the phone with Rainie Stevens—you've been poking into Peter's death?"

"I'm a taxpayer, Jack. I'm allowed to ask questions about a crime that was committed in my jurisdiction."

"Stop it, Carlotta. Let this go—now."

She frowned. "Is that an order, Jack?"

He heaved a sigh, and she could picture him pulling his hand down his face. "No, it's a request. I know you're upset about Peter, but please, I'm asking you to leave this alone and let me handle it."

"Do you have any leads on Walt Tully's whereabouts?"

"That's none of your business… but no. He'll make a mistake and that's when we'll get him." He grunted. "On another topic… have you talked to Wes?"

"Yeah. What do you make of this trafficking theory?"

"Sorry to say it looks legit. They identified the guy Wes alerted us to as a known trafficker. The GBI agents say this happens more than people want to know… and it's rare that victims are recovered. She could be drugged, or controlled… some other way."

She flinched. Ways too horrible to envision.

"It's not a rosy picture," he said, "but no one's giving up hope… yet."

"Neither are we."

"Good. But do me a favor, will you? Go follow Coop around and make *him* crazy for a while, and stay out of police business, okay?"

She frowned. "Okay."

He ended the call and she stuck her tongue out at him. Cretin.

As if it was now Coop's job to manage her.

She worked her mouth back and forth. If Walt Tully had arranged for Peter's death at the Fulton County jail, then chances were he—like Randolph and Peter had both theorized—was still somewhere in the area.

When Randolph was on the run, he'd maintained contact with one person, on and off—*her*. His daughter. No one knew better how strong the father-daughter bond could be. So if Walt Tully was still in the area and needed an ally...

She picked up the phone and called Hannah, who answered on the first ring.

"Hiya. What's up?"

"Hi, Mama. Can I borrow your van for a few hours?"

*****

Carlotta sat in the parking lot of a high-end nail salon, waiting for Tracey Tully Lowenstein to emerge. She was listening to podcasts to pass the time, but surveillance was highly overrated. She'd trailed Tracey from her home in Buckhead to the country club to drop off decorations, to the yoga studio, to a café where she'd lunched with a friend, and finally to the nail salon.

She theorized if Tracey was aiding and abetting her father, her doctor husband didn't know about it, so chances were she'd be connecting with her father when Freddy wasn't around. And from the lateness of the afternoon, Carlotta guessed this would be one of Tracey's last stops before going home to spend the evening with her hubby.

The door opened and Tracey walked out of the salon, blowing on her nails. Carlotta was struck by the fact that when Tracey wasn't being snide, she had such a pretty face. It was interesting to watch her when she didn't know she was being observed.

When Tracey pulled out of the parking lot, Carlotta followed her, expecting her to turn toward her own home. But when Tracey drove into a questionable part of town, Carlotta's interest was piqued. Staying two or three cars behind her, Carlotta watched Tracey's car like a hawk. When the woman's car turned down a side road into a townhome community, Carlotta kept up with her.

She seemed to have a destination in mind—her turns were

deliberate. Then her brake lights came on and she drove by a townhome, her car barely moving. From behind, Carlotta saw Tracey's head turn toward the townhouse, her neck craned, as if she were looking for someone.

Or checking on someone?

Carlotta made note of the address, then when Tracey sped up and left the neighborhood, she did the same. As she suspected, Tracey then drove to her own home, one of the few grand old neighborhoods that wasn't gated, thank goodness. Carlotta drove on by, conceding it might take a few days of surveillance to determine if Tracey was in touch with her father.

But she was good at this.

CHAPTER 23

THE NEXT day was like *Groundhog Day*, following Tracey from her home to the club, to the yoga studio, to a café to lunch with a different friend, then to a salon—this time a hair salon. Carlotta had been waiting for over two hours and was longing for Hannah's company. Too bad she was too busy eating elaborate meals in front of lonely food voyeurs to come along on a stakeout.

But finally the door opened and Tracey emerged, newly coiffed. Again, she expected the woman to turn toward her own home, but instead, Tracey drove back to the same shabby townhome community where she'd gone the day before.

To cruise by the same little townhome at a snail's pace, clearly looking for something—a signal? Suddenly a light came on outside the door of the townhome. At the same time, Tracey pulled away, out of sight, then turned and doubled-back…. and stopped on the opposite side of the street behind two parked cars. Carlotta lifted her binoculars to bring the woman into focus…

Only to find Tracey was also using binoculars.

She dropped down in the seat lest the woman spot her, then peeked back over the dashboard of the van. Tracey was definitely watching the townhome, and Carlotta suspected the outside light was some kind of secret code. There were no cars parked at the residence.

Walt Tully was probably in the townhome at this very moment!

She reached for her phone and connected to Jack's number.

"Hi, Carlotta, what's wrong?'

She frowned. "Why do you assume something's wrong? Something could be right."

"Please," he said, "make my day."

"Only if you promise not to yell at me."

"I'll do no such thing. What the hell are you into now?"

"I've been following Tracey Tully for a couple of days—"

"Are you kidding me?"

"—and right now she's sitting across from a townhome she's been cruising by every day, using binoculars. The outside light just came on… I think Walt Tully is inside, and I think the light is some kind of signal."

"This is crazy, Carlotta."

"To think a daughter would be helping her fugitive father? How many other leads have you gotten on Walt Tully today?"

He sighed. "Where are you?"

She gave him the address. "I'm in Hannah's white van."

"Jesus Christ, no matter what happens, don't get out of that van!"

She ended the call, then lifted her binoculars again. Tracey was still watching the townhouse.

Carlotta surveyed the house—very nondescript, close to Tracey's own neighborhood—the perfect place for her fugitive father to hide out. She scanned the windows for several long minutes, looking for any signs of movement, hoping she'd get lucky and Walt Tully would show his face. Then a curtain at the top window twitched. She gasped and focused on it. Someone was definitely inside, standing by a window, which wasn't normal behavior… unless the person inside was waiting for a visitor.

Suddenly the passenger side door of the van opened. She screamed, then stopped when she realized Jack had scrambled inside.

He frowned at her. "Why don't you blow the horn, too?"

"What took you so long?"

"I couldn't get the department's helicopter," he said dryly.

"It's that house," she said, pointing. She passed him her binoculars. "Someone's inside, at the top window. I saw the curtain move."

He nodded. "I saw it move, too. But that doesn't mean it's Walt Tully."

"But it has to be!"

Jack glanced in the side mirror. "Here comes a black car, tinted windows, driving slowly."

The car rolled past them, then turned into the driveway of the townhome and pulled under a carport.

Her heart was beating wildly. "What if that's Walt?"

"If Walt is driving, then who's in the house?"

As they watched, a man got out of the car holding a bag of take-out food from a pricey restaurant.

"Is it Walt?" she asked. "Can you see?"

"He doesn't look tall enough to be Walt. Maybe it's just a food delivery guy."

But he was acting suspiciously, glancing all around. When he turned his head their way, Carlotta grunted in recognition. "It's Freddy."

"Who's Freddy?"

"Tracey's husband, Dr. Frederick Lowenstein. Maybe he's in on it, bringing Walt meals."

The door suddenly opened and a figure appeared, greeting him exuberantly.

Jack made a rueful noise. "Not unless Walt is disguised as a busty blonde wearing a pink T-shirt and thong." He handed back the binoculars. "Congratulations, Carlotta. You just followed a woman who was following her husband to his mistress's house."

Carlotta winced. "Sorry?"

Jack sat and looked at her, shaking his head. He covered his mouth, then uncovered it, then covered it again. He rubbed his eyes with his palms. He massaged the bridge of his nose and his temples.

Then he climbed out of the van and slammed the door.

CHAPTER 24

WES REACHED down to still his jumping knee. He couldn't blow this deal now with a tell any Grandma bridge player could spot.

Jade had achieved the impossible—found them a sweet card game with a big pot at the sprawling home of an NFL player who lived in the Atlanta suburbs. He'd heard of these private games with crazy pots, but he'd never been invited to one. And from the way the beefy footballers were eyeing Jade, he could guess why she'd been admitted. She'd secured a seat for Wesley she'd said, by assuring everyone he was a rich tech whiz-kid, and had ordered Wes to dress the part. From the back of his closet he'd pulled a stack of designer clothes Carlotta had bought for him and he'd never worn, and had managed to show up with enough conspicuous labels to impress Jade, so he guessed he'd pulled it off.

He looked like a complete douchebag.

The house's great room had been converted into a poker room with five tournament quality tables, ten seats at each. The buy-in was five thousand a pop, so a quarter of a million dollars was making its way through the room tonight. The cashier was located at the center of room, he assumed so everyone could keep an eye on the cashbox and protect it if someone tried to rob them. If he and Jade played their cards right—literally—they could each walk out with a nice payday for the evening.

They'd arrived separately, but pretended to be casually

acquainted. Most of the players looked to be fellow athletes and friendly with each other, but there were doctors and lawyers and real estate developers mixed in. The booze was flowing freely, but Jade had taught him how to make it look as if he was keeping up with everyone else, but stay stone-cold sober while they slowly got sloshed.

Their preparations had been meticulous. Jade had purchased a pair of high-quality infrared glasses with his prescription for him to wear during the game. To the average person, they looked like regular eyeglasses, but when he looked through them, he could see marks of invisible ink that Jade would use to mark the picture cards and aces. At first she'd invented a bracelet to utilize a tiny ink marker, but then had devised an ingenious plan to load one of her false fingernails with the ink, so she could mark the cards with a simple tap.

She would mark the cards, he would play the cards. The plan wasn't to win the overall pot and draw too much attention—they'd be happy walking out with enough to cover the buy-in that Jade had put down, and net Wes twenty grand for his cut. It was, he'd decided, the bare minimum he needed to get to Europe, and if he netted a little extra tonight, it would be a bonus.

They needed to win one of the five tables that was worth fifty grand. Once Wes made it to the final table, he would ease out of the game early and they'd make their getaway.

When he started to get a gnaw of guilt in his gut, he reminded himself why he was doing this—for Meg. Plus it wasn't as if any of these people were hard-up—he and Jade weren't stealing anyone's rent money.

The owner of the house was a big, magnanimous guy who'd apparently been left in charge of a handful of rambunctious kids, mostly boys, who were dressed up like soldiers and wielding Nerf guns and water pistols. Normally Wes didn't like the distraction of having rugrats running in and out, but he appreciated that the dad let his kids play and have fun. He'd never had that with his dad when he was little.

He was antsy for the game to start, but he knew the key to getting out of there with their bounty and no one the wiser was to be super cool and laid back. Jade had given him a beta blocker when they'd arrived to take the edge off without compromising any of his reflexes. The bandages had allowed his fingers to heal enough to handle the cards with confidence.

By the time the host announced the game would begin, they were an hour past the scheduled start time... and everyone was nice and buzzy. Jade sat at his table, a couple of seats to his left. He made it a point never to watch her hands—a dead giveaway, she'd said, that they were in cahoots, so he wasn't sure when she'd started marking cards. But when he saw the first marked card—a queen—his dick jumped.

He casually glanced around the table to see if anyone else had noticed—after all if they were cheating, someone else could be, too—but everyone seemed chill and jovial as the night proceeded. He yukked it up with the guys next to him by pretending he was Meg's friend Marky Mark for the evening—laughing at the right times and making jokes, acting as if the money was easy-come, easy go.

Jade played well, but eventually left the table to let him run with the cards. Suddenly it was down to only four players at his table, then three, then him and another guy, who was, Wes recalled, a friend of the host.

When he realized he was only a few hands away from having the money he needed, adrenaline started to pump through his veins. He got a hard-on. He almost felt sorry for the other guy who was playing blind, holding a lone ace with no idea that Wes had four jacks—two in his hand and two in the community cards that had yet to be revealed. But the guy was feeling the pressure of performing in front of his buds, so he was sweating his bets.

The band of kids broke into the room, jumping and shooting and yelling as if they were launching an attack. As the kids darted around the room, the players were yelling encouragement. Two kids circled his table, firing Nerf guns at each other.

"Okay, okay, keep it down," his opponent said to one of the kids, who appeared to be his son. The little boy, wearing full-on soldier getup, hung on his dad.

"Can I watch?"

"Sure."

The little boy pointed to the cards on the table. "What do the squiggly lines mean?"

Wes looked up, then realized the kid was wearing night

goggles—infrared glasses. His gaze met Jade's across the room. She made a tiny head movement toward the door.

"What do you mean, son?" the guy asked.

Wes coughed. "Dude, I need a bathroom break."

"Go ahead," the guy said, then turned back to his son.

Wes put down his cards, then eased toward the exit. But he knew the minute the guy looked through his son's goggles and realized he'd been played.

"Hey!" he shouted. "The nerdy white guy is cheating! He's marking the cards!"

Pandemonium broke loose. Wes made a run for it, but was brought up short by a guy whose arm was bigger than Wes's chest. He managed to duck the first punch, but the second one caught him between the shoulder blades and took him down. At some point while he was being stomped, another commotion broke out, with someone screaming the cash box was gone, and the white-haired bitch had taken it.

Wes couldn't be mad at her—she'd said if he got caught he would be on his own.

And he had a feeling even if he lived through this, he'd never see Jade again.

CHAPTER 25

CARLOTTA NEARLY suspended surveilling Tracey the following day because she felt so bad her husband was cheating on her. It had to cut deeply that Freddy didn't like her in pink, but apparently was fine if his girlfriend paraded around in it.

In the end, though, she was hoping to bring Walt Tully to justice and if he had something to do with Peter's murder, make him pay. And she still believed the way to find Walt was through a trusted friend or relative.

And daughters were the ultimate daddy-pleasers.

As she could attest.

So she spent a third day rattling around in Hannah's van, following Tracey from her home to the club for a tennis game, then to lunch with her partner. She was wondering what salon Tracey would choose today when the woman veered into the parking lot of a grocery. Carlotta groaned—another hour of waiting. When Tracey finally emerged with two bags of groceries, she loaded them into her car, then made a trip through the pharmacy drive-through.

For antibiotics and anti-virals to ward off STDs? One could hope.

Next she hit the liquor store, and Carlotta couldn't blame her for that.

While she waited for Tracey to exit, she ruminated again over how she'd been so envious of the lives of the people she'd gone to high school with, the ones whose parents hadn't abandoned them. Yet fast forward and so many of them were miserable. Given the chance, she wouldn't trade her problems for theirs.

Tracey came out carrying an enormous bottle of vodka and a jumbo box of wine.

Good girl, Carlotta cheered. Enough alcohol to embalm Freddy.

Since the woman was laden with groceries, she expected Tracey to turn toward her own home. Instead Tracey headed toward the interstate going north. Intrigued, Carlotta followed, keeping a careful distance. By and by she realized Tracey's destination was Lake Lanier, the large man-made reservoir that boasted many marinas and lakefront property. Perhaps the Lowensteins had a weekend home. Jack had said the family residences were being monitored, but the police couldn't be everywhere all the time.

Tracey exited from the interstate and took a winding route before turning into Redbird Marina. The traffic was sparse here, so following her took more care. Carlotta hung back, barely keeping Tracey's vehicle in view, following her into a large mostly-empty parking lot for the marina. Apparently weekdays weren't prime time for boating. Tracey parked, then secured a rolling cart and loaded her groceries and liquor inside. When she headed toward the marina with supplies in tow, Carlotta hastily parked and followed at a distance. She didn't want to spook her now.

Indeed, Tracey was looking all around, as if she was afraid someone was watching. Carlotta's vital signs had ticked up, but she remembered too well the false alarm from the previous day.

Jack might never trust her again.

Tracey wheeled the cart toward the many-pronged floating dock where boats of all sizes were moored. The blue-black water stretched far and wide, big and deep enough for white caps. Someone who looked official checked something in Tracey's hand, then allowed her entry. After that she disappeared from sight among the boats.

Carlotta thought fast, then ran back to the van to pillage Hannah's supplies. She found a bottle of wine that would suffice, then hurried back to the dock. With a groan she realized she wasn't dressed for boating in her denim miniskirt and toeless leather boots. Along the way, though, she spotted an abandoned hat with a boat logo on it in the parking lot, and scooped it up to wear. When she reached the person at the dock who was checking credentials, she offered him a big smile.

"Hi, there. Can you help me? I lost my friend Tracey." She held up the wine. "We left this in the car and she sent me back to get it. But now I don't remember which slip is hers. Am I in the right place?"

"Oh, Ms. Lowenstein who was just here?"

"Yes, that's my friend Tracey."

He checked a list, then smiled. "Slip three fifteen. Down this walkway, then take a right. It's a cabin cruiser."

"Right," Carlotta said. "Thank you so much."

She hurried down the walkway, keeping an eye out for Tracey. When she found slip three fifteen, she pursed her mouth in admiration at the boat sitting there—it was at least thirty-five feet long and since the guy had called it a cabin cruiser, she assumed that mean the door next to the steering wheel led down into a cabin that would be suitable for living.

Or hiding out.

She hung back and waited several long minutes until the door opened. Tracey emerged and shut the door behind her, but not before Carlotta had seen someone else moving inside. Walt Tully?

Tracey checked a buoy between the boat and the dock, then opened the door again and disappeared inside.

Carlotta bit her lip. Should she call Jack? She didn't want to cry wolf again. For all she knew, Tracey could be having her own fling, and meeting her boyfriend here. Or it could be Freddy, and they were reconciling. If only she could see inside.

Then she noticed the portholes. If she could get close enough, she could look into the portholes from the dock without boarding the boat.

Whoever was inside might see her... but she didn't see another choice unless she hung out here all day, hoping they would reveal themselves.

She took a deep breath and edged toward the boat, poised to run if the cabin door opened. She wanted to hang on to the wine bottle in case she needed a weapon, but she abandoned it to have both arms free to balance herself on the bobbing dock. Wobbling, she crept closer and closer to the boat. Then she leaned forward and pressed her face to the porthole, cupping her hand over her eyes. She wasn't sure what she was looking into, so it took her a few seconds to identify that two people were moving around.

The man swung his head in her direction—Walt Tully.

But he saw her, too, and shouted, raising the alarm. Carlotta pulled back, then yanked her phone from her pocket and yelled to her digital assistant, "Call Jack." To her relief the call was transmitted. "Answer, Jack... answer... answer."

"Now what's wrong?" Jack demanded.

"Walt Tully, RedBird Marina, slip three fifteen—hurry!"

The boat cabin door opened and Tracey and Walt charged out.

"You bitch!" Tracey screamed. "Did you follow me?"

Carlotta put out her hands and blocked the walkway. "The police are on their way. It would be better for you both if you just wait until they get here, and don't try to flee." She looked at Walt Tully. "Again."

His face twisted. "I can't believe you'd do this to me, Carlotta. I'm your and Wesley's godfather."

"Only in name," Carlotta said. "You never even looked in on us when Randolph and Valerie left."

He at least had the good grace not to refute her.

She looked to Tracey. "You've been hiding him all this time?"

Tracey nodded, her face murderous. "You should understand better than anybody why I'm doing this. Wouldn't you do anything for your father?"

Carlotta thought of Randolph and how he'd raised her as his own when he didn't have to. She nodded. "I would. That's why the police will go easy on you, Tracey. Just give yourself up."

"Not a chance," Walt shouted. "I can't go to prison—I'd die there."

"You mean like Peter?" Carlotta asked.

"Get out of our way," Tracey yelled, then shoved Carlotta hard.

Not that it took much of a push to send her over the edge of the bobbing dock. She flailed spectacularly, then fell face first into the cold water.

She opened her eyes and moved her arms, waiting to stop sinking, then realized in horror her Vince Camuto booties were not made for swimming. She clawed furiously to reach the surface she could see above her, but was getting nowhere. She struggled to unzip the boots, but they wouldn't budge. She thought of all her loved ones and how she would miss them. And the man whose face was uppermost in her oxygen-deprived mind—

An arm came around her from behind, then dragged her up to the surface. She broke the water sputtering and coughing.

"I got you," Jack said into her ear. "Just breathe."

Within a few strokes, he had her back to the dock. He put his hand under her behind and pushed her up. She flopped over on her back and stared at the sky, wheezing. Jack's face appeared over hers, his mouth set in a grim line. "Are you okay?"

She nodded. "I think so. Walt and Tracey?"

"Secured," he said. "Can you sit up?"

She allowed him to pull her up. "How did you get here so fast?"

"Don't worry about that. Can you stand?"

"I think so."

He helped her to her feet and she leaned on him, still wobbly. He led her down the walkway, and she was thrilled to find her ditched phone, safe and dry.

A few yards away, Tracey and Walt stood with a uniformed Department of Natural Resources officer, their hands handcuffed behind their backs.

"This is your fault, Carlotta," Walt raved at her as they passed. "They're going to get me now."

Tracey shot eye-daggers at her.

"What's he talking about?" Carlotta asked.

"Who knows?" Jack said. "Sometimes fugitives start planting their insanity defense as soon as they're arrested.

She smiled up at him. "Thanks for coming, Jack."

He stopped to face her, then lifted his hand to push a wet strand of hair out of her eyes. "I will always come for you, no matter what."

"Jack…" She pressed her lips together and weighed the words before she said them.

"What? Are you going to tell me you were right again?"

She exhaled, then gave a little laugh and nodded. "How did you know?"

"Because we've been here before."

An understatement of gigantic proportions.

He dipped his chin. "Okay... you were right... again. This time." Then he winked. "Let's get you some dry clothes."

CHAPTER 26

WES OPENED the door to E.'s office and slipped inside.

She looked up, then did a double-take. "What happened to you?"

Long sleeves and long pants concealed most of the bruises he'd received from the beating, but he couldn't do much about the ones on his face. He gingerly lowered himself into a chair. "Bike accident."

She looked dubious, then sighed. "I've been keeping up with news about your girlfriend, Wes. I'm so sorry. I hope the police locate her soon."

He nodded. "So do I."

"I understand you went to the morgue to talk to Coop?"

"Yeah. Now if only the courts would get their act together and get my charges settled and my ankle bracelet removed."

A little furrow appeared on her brow. "Wes... I made a call to the D.A.'s office, like you asked. They said they were ready weeks ago to have your hearing, but last week your attorney asked for a continuance."

"A continuance?"

"A postponement. He said he needed more time to prepare."

A slow boil started in Wes's stomach, then rose like a tide into his lungs, then crowded his throat. All this time his father had been acting as if he was pulling strings for him—he was pulling strings all right—Randolph was the puppet master.

Wes painfully pushed to his feet. "Excuse me."

He left her office and walked back through the waiting room, out into the sun. Then he threw his head back and bellowed like a madman, trying to discharge some of the hurt and anger festering inside him.

Suddenly a hand clasped his shoulder. He stopped, then looked up to see Mouse standing there, his big face concerned.

"Hey, Little Man. You okay?"

Wes's entire body shook. "No... I'm not okay. I gotta find Meg. I gotta bring her home."

Mouse smiled. "Relax. Good news—I got that passport you asked for." He held out an envelope.

Wes wanted to cry. "I appreciate it, man, but I don't have the money."

"Already paid for."

"Mouse, I can't let you do that."

The big man raised his hands. "Wasn't me. A friend of yours contacted me, wanted to pay for it."

He frowned. "Who?"

"Someone named Jade, said she owed you one."

He'd told her why he needed the cash. She must've had a crisis of conscience on her way out of town with the cashbox from the game.

Mouse put the envelope in his hand. "Go find your girl."

Wes bit back tears of relief. "Okay. I will. Thanks, man."

Mouse walked back to his car, then drove off with a wave.

After wiping his eyes, Wes opened the envelope and removed the passport. It looked authentic. He smiled. One step at a time.

But first, he had to talk to his dad. He punched in Randolph's number and he answered right away.

"Wes... where are you?"

"You son of a bitch. You had my attorney ask for a *postponement*?"

Randolph was silent, then he sighed. "It was for your own good, Wes, believe me."

"I don't believe anything you say," Wes ground out. "Do me a favor, and don't do me any more favors. *Ever*."

He ended the call, then phoned Chance.

"Hey, dude, what's up?"

"I need to borrow some money, enough for a plane ticket to Europe. Can you spot me?"

"Yeah, dude, sure. Hannah's got some kind of new business going, is making cash hand over fist. Whatever you need."

"Thanks, man, really. See you soon." He ended the call, feeling a tiny bit closer to Meg.

CHAPTER 27

CARLOTTA MADE her way across the cemetery to a newly dug grave mounded high with fading flowers. The granite headstone had already been erected. *Peter Ashford, Beloved Son and Friend*

Tears clogged her throat as she lay a bouquet of white roses on the mound. She still couldn't believe he was gone, it would take some time to sink in. Her chest ached for the uselessness of his death. Even if Peter had been sentenced to prison time, she felt sure he would've spent it wisely, trying to right the wrongs he'd committed. It wasn't fair that his life had been cut short, and in such an ugly way.

Jack said at this point Peter's murder couldn't be tied to Walt Tully, but they were still digging.

"I will get you justice," she whispered.

The breeze picked up, lifting her hair and sending petals from the flowers airborne, swirling and dancing. She smiled, feeling as if she'd gotten the message he'd wanted her to have.

I am free... and so are you... go live your life... be happy...

Suddenly in the mood to celebrate, she walked back through the graveyard, then called a ride-share service to Moody's.

On the short ride over, she luxuriated in the beautiful weather they were having. Big puffy clouds rolled across a turquoise sky. She sent up a prayer that Wes's girlfriend would be rescued soon, and others in her grim situation. Wes had taken a nasty spill on his bike, so he was taking a break from the driving range. She hoped his heart would heal along with his body, although she knew it would take a while.

When she walked into Moody's she was delighted to see the owner herself serving drinks and selling stogies behind the bar on the first floor. June Moody was dressed in a black ponte skirt and fitted white cotton shirt with heels, classy, as usual. Her face lit up when she saw Carlotta.

"Long time, no see," June said. "What have you been up to?"

Carlotta laughed. "New things."

June poured two shots of top-shelf tequila and handed one to Carlotta. "To new things."

She tossed back the shot, pleasantly warmed when it burned all the way down.

"Another?" June asked.

"Sure," Carlotta said.

She looked past June to see a picture of Colleen Mason, the redhead who'd claimed she'd had an affair with Senator Reeder, on the screen."

"Such a shame," June said.

"What happened?"

"She committed suicide, poor girl." June turned up the volume.

"A representative for Senator Max Reeder describes Colleen Mason as 'a deeply disturbed woman who has come to an untimely end.' He sends condolences to her family."

Carlotta gasped. "I met her."

"When?"

"I talked to her in the TSA security line once at the Atlanta airport... we were on the same plane. It was just a chance encounter... and now she's dead."

June pointed to the empty shot glasses. "Another?"

"Keep 'em coming," Carlotta said. The alcohol was already starting to work its way into her bloodstream. Over the next hour, she caught June up on things going on in her life, and hoped someday she and Valerie would have the same easy camaraderie.

"And guess what—Hannah's pregnant!"

"This should be interesting," June said with a laugh. Then she angled her head. "And things are good between you and Coop?"

"Not as good as they could be," Carlotta admitted. "And

that's my fault." Then she smiled, feeling sparkly around the edges. "But I'm going to change that... soon."

"Here's your chance," June said, then nodded to the door.

Carlotta turned to see Coop walking in. She grinned. "Hey, you."

He looked amused. "Hey, you. How many of those have you had?"

"Several," she admitted.

He looked to June. "Thanks for calling."

"You bet."

He slid onto the stool next to Carlotta. "Rough day?"

She nodded. "I went to Peter's grave."

He picked up her hand and intertwined their fingers. "I'm sorry."

She sighed. "Me too. But at least Walt Tully is in custody."

He grinned. "Jack owes you for that one."

"Jack thinks like a cop. I think like a daughter."

"You and Randolph do have quite a connection."

She nodded, then reached up to finger the locket around her neck.

"How about I take you home?" he suggested.

"With you?" she asked.

A fire ignited in his brown eyes. "That sounds good to me."

She waved to June, then held on to Coop's arm as he led her out the door and to his Corvette. The warm, cloudy day had turned into a humid night with the scent of rain in the fresh air. She felt young and vibrant, like when she and Peter were just falling in love. The drive gave her time to study Coop's profile and to imagine what their life together would be like. Fun, she decided. Carefree. Full of laughter.

The one thing that kept pulling her back to Jack was their strong physical attraction and sexual history. Coop couldn't compete with that unless they established their own physical bond. It was past time to get naked with this man.

When they reached his industrial condo, Coop parked the 'Vette, then helped her out. She could feel the anticipation vibrating between them as he unlocked the door to his home. She'd been to his place before, but she'd never spent the night.

When they walked in, she reacquainted herself with the space that had once been a mechanic's garage, complete with roll-up door. Like Coop himself, the place was artsy and cool and unique.

"And where is your bedroom?"

"It's upstairs," he said with a grin. "Still want to see it?"

She lifted her hand and traced the outline of his endearing, handsome face. "I need to tell you something first."

"What's that?"

"I love you, Coop."

His lips parted, then he looked apprehensive. "You're tipsy, Carlotta. I'm not sure you know what you're saying."

"I know what I'm saying. I needed a little liquid courage to say it. I love you. When Peter died it made me realize how short life can be."

His expression transformed to elation, then he pulled her into his arms. "I love you, too. So much."

"Then take me upstairs."

"You don't have to ask twice."

He lifted her into his arms and carried her up the stairs, then kicked open his bedroom door and lay her on his bed. They tore at each others' clothes and in the space of a few seconds were naked and lying against each other. He was long and lean and finely muscled, with broad shoulders and a planed torso. Coop kissed her deeply, running his hands over her breasts and stomach, inserting his fingers into her folds to strum her to a hum. She sank her teeth into his shoulder while he urged her to greater heights. When she cried out his name, he kissed her neck and laved her nipples. She rode the wave of bliss, feeling cherished and protected. And she wanted to experience all of him.

She shifted under him, burning with the anticipation of having him inside her.

"Are you going to remember this in the morning?" he asked breathlessly.

She smiled. "If not, we can do it again."

With that, he thrust inside her, filling her completely. They found a deep, slow rhythm, but it wasn't long until she was climbing the crest again, while he was straining to hold off.

"I can't take much more," he murmured.

"Now," she whispered.

They came together in a crashing wave of longing and delayed desire, clinging to each other. At last... at long last.

CHAPTER 28

"I MIGHT be gone for a while," Wes said to Einstein. "Carlotta wouldn't mind if you starved to death, but I'll get Coop to feed you."

In the aquarium on the other side of his bedroom, his python lifted and lowered its head, its forked tongue darting in and out. He was typically more active in the evening hours, and darkness had fallen early due to a cloudy sky.

Wes glanced out the window, hoping the cloud cover didn't delay his flight to Dublin. He wanted to be on the ground by morning looking for Meg.

His heart pounded double-time as he pulled his duffel bag from under his bed. Into it went his sturdiest pair of shoes, extra socks and underwear, and shirts to layer if the temperatures were cooler than in Atlanta. He went to his bookshelf to find something to read on the plane.

His hand hovered over the *Study Guide for the ACT College Entrance Exam* and *Study Guide for the SAT College Entrance Exam* Mouse had given him. The big man had always come through for him. Mouse seemed to understand him better than his own father.

Opting for lighter fare and a lighter load, he pulled the worn copy of *The Catcher in the Rye* from his shelf and pushed it into a side pocket, along with a detailed map of Ireland and Northern Ireland. He'd buy more maps when he got there if he had to. Who knew where her abductor had taken her?

When panic rose in his chest, threatening to suffocate him, he gulped deep breaths. If someone had taken her, it meant she was alive, and that was something to hang on to. When his mind drifted into the dark places of what they could be doing to her, he jerked it back. For now he had to concentrate on one thing at a time, and right now that was getting through TSA security with a fake passport and getting on that plane. He hoped the makeup he'd lifted from Carlotta's bathroom and applied to his face was enough to cover the bruises convincingly.

He stuffed half the cash Chance had given him into his wallet and the other half into the pocket of his cargo pants, then clipped his phone to his belt and stowed his charger. As he zipped up his bag, he was sure he'd forgotten lots of things, but reasoned he could buy necessities once he landed.

He checked his watch—might as well leave now to give himself plenty of time to practice his bullshitting skills in case someone questioned his documentation. Plus every minute he delayed he risked Carlotta coming home and he really didn't want to deal with her right now. After he landed would be soon enough to let her and his parents know what he'd done.

He propped his leg on his bed, then used a pair of tin snips to cut through the thick black rubber of the ankle monitor. It fell to the floor with a dull thud, red light blinking.

He turned off his bedroom light, then headed toward the front door, rehashing his travel plans. The walk to the Lindbergh station would take ten minutes, another ten minutes to wait for a southbound train, then thirty minutes or so to get to the airport.

When he turned to lock the front door, the flash of headlights swept over him. His stomach sank, but when he turned he was already practicing a lie in his head about spending the night with Chance.

Except it wasn't Carlotta—it was his dad.

And when Randolph climbed out of his SUV, Wes could tell from the look on his face that he knew what was going down.

Chance had ratted him out, dammit.

"Wes, don't do this," Randolph said.

"I can't do nothing," Wes said in a choked voice. "I have to go look for her."

"Leave it to the professionals, you're only going to make things worse for yourself."

"I don't care," Wes said, leaping off the steps. "And I don't expect you to understand because you don't give a damn about anyone but yourself." He wiped away hot tears before they could fall. "All that time I thought you were trying to help me clear the charges, and instead you were telling the attorney to delay everything. To keep me here where you could control me."

Randolph pressed his lips together. "It's true I wanted to keep you here, but it's not for the reason you think. I want what's best for you, Wes, I really do."

"I don't believe you anymore," Wes said hoarsely. "You lie and you do what's best for *you*."

Randolph's face was stony, unreadable. "I can't let you leave. If you get caught, Kelvin Lucas will be happy for a legitimate reason to toss you in the state pen."

"Because I'm your son," Wes said bitterly. "I'm starting to learn that being your son has no upside."

His father's jaw hardened. "I'm sorry you feel that way. But you're not leaving."

"Watch me." Wes strode toward the street, walking past Randolph.

His father's hand reached out to snag his arm.

Without thinking about it, Wes balled up his fist and swung. Pain exploded through his hand when it connected with his father's jaw. Randolph staggered back, stunned. Then he lifted his hands. "Okay. I'm not stopping you."

Wes was just as surprised by the punch as his father. But he kept walking, shaking his fingers, wondering if he'd broken his hand. But feeling great about standing up for himself.

When he reached the sidewalk, his phone rang. He checked it, expecting Chance to be calling to apologize for ratting him out. Instead Mark's name flashed on the screen.

Wes connected the call with his throbbing hand, steeling himself for the worst.

"This is Wes."

After a few seconds of silence, a small voice sounded. "Wes... it's Meg."

His heart vaulted and he could barely speak. "Meg? Meg!

Are you okay? Where are you?"

"I'm okay," she said. "I'm with my father... and Mark."

"What happened?"

"I was rescued."

"By the police?"

"I thought so, but now the police are acting as if they don't know what happened. The man disappeared after he dropped me at my father's hotel, but when we were in the car, I overheard him talking to someone on the phone, and the person called him Birch."

Wes's mouth fell open while his brain tried to fit all the pieces together. Birch, his dad's bodyguard and sidekick from Vegas, with the military background and obscure job title.

His dad had been keeping him here because he was taking care of things.

"I can't talk now," she said. "But I'll call again soon. And Wes?"

"Yeah?"

"I love you."

Before he could respond, the call ended. Still trying to process what had transpired, Wes turned to walk back to his Dad, his feet slowly gathering speed.

When he rounded the corner, Randolph was standing next to his SUV, looking defeated.

"Dad?"

Randolph lifted his head.

Wes ran to him and tackled him with a bear hug. "Thank you. I'm sorry, Dad. Thank you."

Randolph pulled back with a little smile. "What's this about?"

"Meg's okay. She was rescued... and she knows the man's name was Birch."

Randolph's face went still. Then he wet his lips. "I'm glad she's safe, son. But you can't tell a soul Birch was involved, and you need to tell Meg the same thing, do you understand?"

Wes frowned. "Not really."

"No one can know what happened—no one. This will be our secret, okay? Promise me."

A faint feeling of unease nudged him, but Wes was so happy, he pushed it away. "Okay... I promise."

CHAPTER 29

CARLOTTA SHIFTED the Miata into higher gear and headed north, lifting her face to the sun and reveling in the feel of the wind through her hair.

"How does she handle?" Coop shouted from the passenger seat.

She grinned. "Better even than I remember."

He gave her a thumb's up then settled back in his seat, letting her have some private time to reflect... and to remember.

This car had meant the world to her, and so had Randolph. She'd loved him for splurging on her and making her feel so special. It was one of the few things she had to draw on for strength after he and her mother had left. Years later when the car had started giving her problems, it had seemed like a harbinger of bad tidings, a warning that she should forget about her father and get used to the idea of life without her parents. The day it had refused to start had been a low point. She had slumped in the driver's seat and cried for what seemed liked hours, pounding the steering wheel in frustration and futility over the hand life had dealt her. After that she'd wavered between selling the car for desperately needed cash, and hanging onto the last thing that reminded her of the life she'd once had. In the end she hadn't been able to part with it.

And now she didn't know if she wanted to.

Maybe it wasn't right that her parents had kept the truth of her birth from her, but would things have been different if they'd told her? Would she have felt caught between two families and out of place at an age when she was already emotionally fragile? Would it have changed the way she felt about Wes, especially after her parents had left?

No, in hindsight, she was glad they hadn't told her. Because it was her deep longing for Randolph that had driven her to keep looking for them, to track them down in Vegas, and ultimately reunite their family. She couldn't imagine her life now without Prissy. And Valerie might have languished in limbo if they hadn't brought her back to Atlanta where Coop had found her the proper care. And although things were rocky between Wes and Randolph, deep down she knew he was better off having a father around, and in time hopefully they would grow close.

She turned her head to smile at Coop. Her chest felt crowded with love and gratitude. He smiled back, then reached over to cover her hand with his. They rode in companionable silence, enjoying the summer scenery on the two lane road leading to Lake Lanier. A picnic basket sat in the tiny trunk, loaded with sandwiches and bottles of sparkling water. She couldn't imagine a nicer day, or anyone she'd rather spend it with.

For the next several minutes she ran the car through its paces, enjoying its responsiveness around curves and feeling one with the road. When the sign for a picnic area came into view, she slowed, gearing down, and pulled off onto a narrow tree-lined road that led to a pretty grassy area overlooking the lake.

"Looks like we have the place to ourselves," Coop remarked, then wagged his eyebrows.

She laughed, thinking she wouldn't mind rolling around with him on a picnic blanket.

They climbed out and while Coop retrieved the basket, she walked around the convertible, admiring its lines. "Is it wrong to love a car?"

"Not at all. Are you having second thoughts about selling it?"

She pressed her lips together, then gave a little shrug. "Maybe. It's a woman's prerogative to change her mind, isn't it?"

"You know that adage scares men to death, right?"

She laughed again, then followed him to a flat area with enough shade to protect them from the sun. They worked together to spread out a red blanket, then removed the decadent contents of the basket—turkey and brie sandwiches, clumps of juicy grapes, and chunks of dark chocolate, then dug in with gusto. Throughout they shared stories about their day and talked about the good news of Meg's safe return.

"Do you know what happened?" Coop asked.

She shook her head. "Wes said the men who abducted her got spooked and dropped her off at her father's hotel. They got away, but the important thing is she's fine."

"Good news all around," Coop agreed.

At some point Carlotta noticed she hadn't craved a cigarette in a while, then reached to check the nicotine patch on the back of her arm. When her fingers came up empty she realized she'd forgotten to put it on... and she was fine.

Better than fine.

Elation coursed through her to have finally kicked her nasty habit. "What a perfect day," she said on a sigh.

"I can think of only one thing that would make it better," Coop said.

"What's that?" she asked, turning her head toward him. At the sight of the velvet ring box, her breath caught in her lungs.

He opened the lid to reveal a sparkling diamond solitaire. "Say you'll marry me."

Carlotta covered her mouth with her hand as her eyes filled with tears. "Coop."

He angled his head. "Please tell me those are happy tears."

She studied his handsome face, his kind eyes, his beautiful hands, his loving body.

"You're leaving me hanging here," he said gently.

He was a wonderful man, and he would take good care of her heart. She loved him, they would have a fun, happy life together.

Carlotta uncovered her mouth. "Yes. Yes, Coop, I'll marry you. Yes!"

CHAPTER 30

CARLOTTA WHEELED a smart-looking roll-on bag into the lobby of a busy conference hotel in Midtown. She wore a chic pantsuit with comfortable wedges and black sunglasses.

Oh, and an engagement ring.

She walked past the reservations counter to the concierge desk.

"May I help you?" the woman asked.

"I'm looking for the business office."

"On the mezzanine," the woman said, pointing.

"Thank you."

She walked slowly and confidently to the elevator and rode up one level, then located the business office. Inside, she found an unoccupied computer, then pulled up a web browser and accessed the fake email address she'd used to register the semen sample for DNA analysis. When she saw an email from the DNA kit company with the subject line "Congratulations! Here is Your Genetic Profile" she felt a rush of adrenaline. If the profile matched John Smythe or Trevor Biondi, she'd be able to pay an extra fee and plug the sample into the global family tree and hopefully see it match to a relative she could connect to them.

With her heart thumping in her chest, she clicked on the email, then pulled up the genetic profile.

Almost immediately, her heart sank. The ancestry breakdown was ninety-five percent Northwestern Russian, with smaller

Eastern European percentages, and only one percent Asian, one percent North Africa.

The sample didn't belong to the kid calling himself John Smythe nor to Trevor Biondi.

Whoever had left the sample had a predisposition to high cholesterol, one of the handful of medical findings that was listed. Big whoop.

She sat back in the chair, feeling utterly defeated. The condom had apparently been discarded by someone who'd stayed in the hotel room before Patricia, and housecleaning had missed it because it was wedged behind the waste can.

So Patricia's death really had been an accident.

Carlotta crossed her arms and hugged herself, soaking in the truth. Everyone—Jack, Coop, Hannah, Dr. Denton—had been right that she'd concocted a murder mystery around Patricia's death because she didn't want to believe the woman's demise had been so inadvertent. Her own guilt over unkind remarks and deflected overtures had led her on a wild goose chase to prove she was a good person after all. The enormity of her overreach left her breathless.

She was so shaken, she nearly forgot about her own genetic profile. Feeling numb, she logged out, then accessed the second fake address under which she'd registered her own kit. An identical email with the "Congratulations!" subject line sat in the inbox. She hesitated for two long minutes trying to decide if she truly wanted to know her genetic makeup.

Then again, simply knowing her ancestry breakdown wouldn't hurt anyone... and it might illuminate a predisposition to a preventable disease, something more serious than high cholesterol. She owed it to herself to know that much.

She clicked on the link to bring up her profile and scanned the numbers. She was of mostly European ancestry, Scandinavian and Norwegian. In short, there was nothing on the surface to hint at her father's identity. He could've been a childhood friend of her mother's, a high-school crush, a college fling.

A scan of the medical findings showed she had a predisposition to high blood pressure.

Which could easily be a result of her predisposition to meddle.

Carlotta shook her head, perturbed at her own behavior.

Nothing beneficial had come out of this tedious exercise.

She reached for the mouse to click off the report, then spotted a link just below the last line of text.

Add your genetic profile to the worldwide family tree to see if you have DNA matches.

Carlotta hesitated, then moved her mouse to the link. What were the chances, really, that her father or his relatives had both ordered their genetic profiles *and* added them to the worldwide tree? The odds had to be small... right? A shot in the dark.

Besides, clicking the link would only tell her *if* she had DNA matches, not what they were.

She hovered over the link, then clicked. When she was asked to provide payment for the add-on information, she used a generic debit giftcard she'd bought with cash. In a few seconds, the results popped onto the screen.

Matches in Parent/Child: 0

A mixture of relief and disappointment bled through her. Knowing the information wasn't available was satisfying in and of itself. She was done here. She moved the mouse to click off the screen.

Then another result popped onto the screen.

Matches in Immediate Family (full siblings, grandparents, or grandchildren): 0

Again, Carlotta sagged in relief.

Then another result popped onto the screen.

Matches in Close Family (aunt or an uncle, niece or nephew, half-sibling): 1

Her heart thudded against her breastbone. She stared at the number one until her eyes watered. Which was it—an aunt? A nephew? She swallowed hard. A half-sibling?

And from her mother's side, or her father's?

She scanned the screen she was on. At the top, a line of text read "Your Profile Name Other Members Will See." Her profile name defaulted to the first six letters of the fake email address she'd used, JPTYER. If she clicked on the link, no one would know who she was... and she wouldn't know the name of her close family match unless they'd chosen to list it.

With her heart now in her throat, she clicked on the link and waited.

The results popped onto the screen, and the air left Carlotta's lungs.

Tracey Tully Lowenstein.

No... it couldn't be... because that would mean... Walt Tully was her biological father?

As her mind reeled, her hands moved wildly to remove the evidence from the screen—she didn't want to see it.

But now she couldn't unsee it.

Carlotta somehow managed to logoff the site and shut down the session. She pushed to her feet and moved forward, hoping her legs would support her. Feeling raw and tingly, she backtracked to the elevator and pushed the button for the lobby, leaning on the handle of her roll-on to keep from falling down. When the doors opened, she walked in, distantly registering relief to have the car to herself. She forced herself to breathe deeply, to deliver oxygen to her traumatized brain. She stared straight ahead. It felt important to stay very still and to think about anything other than what she'd just learned.

On the wall of the state-of-the-art elevator, a monitor streamed a trendy news program. Clips of Colleen Mason played, presumably in an attempt to milk the woman's suicide in light of her allegations against Senator Max Reeder. It seemed the media was reluctant to relinquish the juicy scandal. Text of the report scrolled across the bottom of the screen, but Carlotta was fixated on something else that had caught her eye: Colleen Mason being met by paparazzi as she left her apartment and dashed to her car. She was carrying a distinctive black makeup bag.

The same one Patricia had taken to Dallas.

On the same flight Colleen Mason had been a passenger on.

Coincidence?

At the moment her mind was too fuzzy to string together the implications, but one truth had long ago imbedded itself in her mind: There was no such thing as coincidence.

-The End-

A NOTE FROM THE AUTHOR

Thank you so very much for reading 11 BODIES MOVING ON! I'm always happy to get back to these characters who feel like family, but this book will always be memorable because I wrote it while self-quarantining during the COVID-19 outbreak. I'm grateful to have had this project to keep my hands and mind busy at such a worrisome time. I sincerely hope you and your loved ones fared well during the crisis.

A shout-out to the following readers for entering my Facebook title contest and submitting the title I ultimately used for this book:

Melissa Lonergan	Shawna Denton
Connie Gallacher	Chandra Petter
Cindy Mendenhall Rosenberg	Janice Tatrow
Dianne Dei Santi	Holly Pirtle
Joanie Bloomfield	Gwen Hansen

Thanks so much, everyone, for brainstorming a title I love! I have the BEST readers a writer could ask for.

If you enjoyed 11 BODIES MOVING ON and you have a few minutes to leave a review at your favorite online bookstore, I would appreciate it very much. Reviews are important because online bookstores use them as a factor for showing a book to readers when they're browsing. And attracting new readers means I can keep writing new stories! Plus I want to know what my readers are thinking. What do you think will happen next? Fyi, there will be at least one more book in the Body Movers series!

And are you signed up to receive notices of my future book releases? If not, please visit www.stephaniebond.com and enter your email address. While you're on my website, check out the FAQs page for more information about the history and the future of the Body Movers series.

Thanks again for your time and interest, and for telling your friends about my books. As long as you keep reading, I'll keep writing!

Happy reading!

Stephanie Bond

OTHER WORKS BY STEPHANIE BOND

Humorous romantic mysteries:
COMEBACK GIRL—*Home is where the hurt is.*
TEMP GIRL—*Change is good... but not great.*
COMA GIRL—*You can learn a lot when people think you aren't listening.*
TWO GUYS DETECTIVE AGENCY—*Even Victoria can't keep a secret from us...*
OUR HUSBAND—*Hell hath no fury like three women scorned!*
KILL THE COMPETITION—*There's only one sure way to the top...*
I THINK I LOVE YOU—*Sisters share everything in their closets...including the skeletons.*
GOT YOUR NUMBER—*You can run, but your past will eventually catch up with you.*
WHOLE LOTTA TROUBLE—*They didn't plan on getting caught...*
IN DEEP VOODOO—*A woman stabs a voodoo doll of her ex, and then he's found murdered!*
VOODOO OR DIE—*Another voodoo doll, another untimely demise...*
BUMP IN THE NIGHT—*a short mystery*

***Body Movers* series:**
PARTY CRASHERS (full-length prequel)
BODY MOVERS
2 BODIES FOR THE PRICE OF 1
3 MEN AND A BODY
4 BODIES AND A FUNERAL
5 BODIES TO DIE FOR
6 KILLER BODIES
6 ½ BODY PARTS (novella)
7 BRIDES FOR SEVEN BODIES
8 BODIES IS ENOUGH
9 BODIES ROLLING
10 BODIES LYING
11 BODIES MOVING ON

Romances:

FACTORY GIRL—*Long hours, low pay, big dreams...*

COVER ME—*A city girl goes country to man-sit a hunky veterinarian who's the victim of a "cover curse"!*

DIAMOND MINE—*A woman helps the one who got away choose a ring—for another woman!*

SEEKING SINGLE MALE (for the holidays)—*A roommate mixup leads to mistletoe mayhem!*

MANHUNTING IN MISSISSIPPI—*She's got a plan to find herself a man!*

TAKING CARE OF BUSINESS—*An FBI agent goes undercover at a Vegas wedding chapel as the Elvis impersonator!*

IT TAKES A REBEL—*A former hotshot athlete is determined to win over the heiress to a department store empire who clashes with the new spokesman—him!*

WIFE IS A 4-LETTER WORD—*A honeymoon for one... plus one.*

ALMOST A FAMILY—*Fate gave them a second chance at love...*

LICENSE TO THRILL—*She's between a rock and a hard body...*

STOP THE WEDDING!—*If anyone objects to this wedding, speak now...*

THREE WISHES—*Be careful what you wish for!*

The Southern Roads series:

BABY, I'M YOURS (novella)

BABY, DRIVE SOUTH

BABY, COME HOME

BABY, DON'T GO

BABY, I'M BACK (novella)

BABY, HOLD ON (novella)

BABY, IT'S YOU (novella)

Nonfiction:

GET A LIFE! 8 STEPS TO CREATE YOUR OWN LIFE LIST—*a short how-to for mapping out your personal life list!*

YOUR PERSONAL FICTION-WRITING COACH: *365 Days of Motivation & Tips to Write a Great Book!*

ABOUT THE AUTHOR

Stephanie Bond was seven years deep into a corporate career in computer programming and pursuing an MBA at night when an instructor remarked she had a flair for writing and suggested she submit material to academic journals. But Stephanie was more interested in writing fiction—more specifically, romance and mystery novels. After writing in her spare time for two years, she sold her first manuscript; after selling ten additional projects to two publishers, she left her corporate job to write fiction full-time. To-date, Stephanie has more than eighty published novels to her name, including the popular BODY MOVERS humorous mystery series, and STOP THE WEDDING!, a romantic comedy adapted into a movie for the Hallmark Channel. Stephanie lives in Atlanta, where she is probably working on a story at this very moment. For more information on Stephanie's books, visit www.stephaniebond.com.

COPYRIGHT INFORMATION